"You're pu_____.

"I'm *treating* yo_____
ambitious goal o_ _____ _____ time frame."

"It's not the exercises, darlin', it's the attitude. You *want* me to hurt."

She took the bull by the horns. "I do not want to hurt you."

He stopped again. "You should. I hurt you."

It took Ruby a moment to decide how to respond.

"Yes, you did." In for a penny, in for a pound. "You hurt me deeply, Luke Buckton."

Luke stopped walking, holding her gaze for a moment. His blue eyes looked like their depths went on forever. "I know that."

"Did you know it when you left? Did you think about it at all?"

"I wouldn't let myself think about it at first. I let all the dreams and the money dangling in front of my face crowd it out."

"You said such…hurtful things."

She heard him sigh. "I needed to burn the bridges behind me. I figured we'd both be better off if you hated me."

"It doesn't work that way, Luke."

Allie Pleiter, an award-winning author and RITA® Award finalist, writes both fiction and nonfiction. Her passion for knitting shows up in many of her books and all over her life. Entirely too fond of French macarons and lemon meringue pie, Allie spends her days writing books and avoiding housework. Allie grew up in Connecticut, holds a BS in speech from Northwestern University and lives near Chicago, Illinois.

Visit the Author Profile page at Harlequin.com for more titles.

The Bull Rider's Homecoming

Allie Pleiter

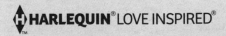

Recycling programs
for this product may
not exist in your area.

LOVE INSPIRED BOOKS

ISBN-13: 978-0-373-89927-2

The Bull Rider's Homecoming

Copyright © 2017 by Alyse Stanko Pleiter

www.Harlequin.com

Printed in U.S.A.

My grace is sufficient for you, for My power is made perfect in weakness.

—*2 Corinthians* 12:9

To physical therapists everywhere
who help so many to heal.

Acknowledgments

There was a heap of technical information to get right in this book, and I had lots of generous help. Dr. David Chen from the Rehabilitation Institute of Chicago always lends his expertise for injuries and their symptoms. Nancy A. Hughes, PT, ICCE, enthusiastically shared her insight and great scene ideas as a physical therapist.
Ed Crowder was kind enough to read the manuscript for bull-riding accuracy. If there are mistakes or misrepresentations in this book, the fault is purely mine, and not in the excellent information they provided me.

Chapter One

Luke Buckton stood on the porch of the Blue Thorn Ranch, his childhood home, disgusted at how he needed to grip the handrail to keep his balance.

Pain came with a life spent trying to stay on top of 1,700 pounds of bucking bull. Every bull rider knew pain went with the territory. Bull riding was dangerous—that's what made it exciting. And profitable, if done right. Sure, you got hurt—everyone got hurt—but you "cowboyed up" after an injury and got back in there, period. Luke hadn't come close to winning the Touring Pro Series championship by paying attention to pain. He ignored it.

The numbness he fought now? That was a whole other kind of enemy. It messed with his mind and defied submission. Luke could ride in pain, could win in pain—he had, in fact, on dozens of occasions. Now, he couldn't always tell where his leg ended and the ground began. He could think "stand" but couldn't feel it, even when he was standing. That threatened his career worse than the largest, meanest bull on earth.

It made him mad. And the anger and frustration made him mean to just about everyone, including his grandmother who'd just come up behind him.

"How are you feeling?" Gran asked as she approached him with a cup of coffee. He'd left six years ago in such a fury of pride and defiance—and had returned home so full of bitterness and dissatisfaction—that he couldn't quite understand how Gran found it possible to be nice to him.

Luke took the coffee and gave Gran the answer he gave everyone: "Better." Most days it wasn't true. It wasn't true today.

His hometown of Martins Gap was as gossipy as a small Texas town could get. In the days and weeks since he'd returned, he'd heard the whispers, caught the rumors and ignored the stares. *Isn't that Luke Buckton, home on the Blue Thorn? Did you see he limps now?*

Luke had always envisioned his eventual return to Martins Gap as the grandest of victory laps—a homecoming for the local golden boy whose future had always been too big for this place. He'd planned to come home a national champion.

If Dad was still alive, wouldn't he have had a field day with how those plans turned out?

Gran sipped her tea. "The new therapist is due about now, isn't she?"

Luke didn't buy his grandmother's sugar-sweet tone. He knew full well Gran wanted to take a switch to him for the way he'd treated the last two therapists they'd sent. It was so clear to Luke they weren't up to the challenge that he'd groused them away in a single session each. He didn't have time or patience to pussyfoot around with careful exercises or gentle treatments. Luke needed to hit this fast and hard so that he could recover and get back to work. Anyone who wasn't on board with that strategy was useless.

Which meant he had a pretty good idea of who was about to come up the drive. Had planned for it, in fact.

He shifted his foot, reaching to feel the give of the porch boards underneath his boot. *Nothing.* It was beyond infuriating. "At ten."

"So…you think it'll be her?" Gran asked, as if it were an innocent question.

Two could play at that game. "Who?" he asked in equally innocent tones.

Gran swatted him. Hard. For eighty-five, that woman could still hold her own. "You know who. Don't think I can't see exactly what you're doing. If you wanted Ruby Sheldon to be your therapist—and I certainly can't imagine why she'd ever agree to such a notion—you should have just asked for her."

As if it were that simple. Luke didn't truly know if he wanted Ruby to be his therapist. He'd hoped there was another way. It'd be much simpler with someone else, that was sure. Only the two others his doctor had sent clearly weren't up to the job, at least not by his estimation. And that left going all the way to Austin to get treatment, or putting up with Ruby.

Putting up with Ruby. As if she was a nagging itch or an uncomfortable chair instead of the biggest regret and saddest chapter of his life. He'd never quite forgiven himself for how he'd broken Ruby's heart, despite six years of steady effort to keep all thoughts of her firmly out of his head. It stuck in his craw to need her help now, and he wasn't sure he could choke that down even if she might be the only person in twenty miles who knew him well enough to get him where he needed to go. "I was hoping to avoid this." He grumbled. "I think I'd rather cut off my leg than give Ruby the chance to order me around."

Gran's eyes narrowed. "Don't you ever talk like that." He knew Gran loved him, but she'd never minced words about what she thought of his choice to leave home to join the bull riding circuit. It didn't matter how good he was at it, or how he rose in the rankings, Gran still thought it "dangerous nonsense that took him away from family" and told him so. Of course, that was only when he bothered to call her, which had been woefully rare until the gut-wrenchingly humble call of "can I come home?" three weeks ago. Had there been any other way…

Had there been any other way, he wouldn't be standing on the Blue Thorn Ranch waiting to see if Ruby Sheldon dared to show up back in his life. Suddenly, he wanted to do this moment on his own terms, not under Gran's scrutiny. "I'll be waiting in the guesthouse." With that, he took his coffee and his cane and made his way across the clearing to the closest thing he had to "his own turf" on Blue Thorn land.

The Blue Thorn Ranch.
Ruby couldn't quite believe she was back

here, about to see Luke Buckton. Funny and sad how life worked in circles.

The physical buildings and layout of the ranch hadn't changed. The big house still boasted the front porch swing where she and Luke had plotted his dazzling rodeo career. The horse barn where he'd first kissed her—a stunning surprise of a kiss she hadn't ever dreamed could really happen—still stood facing west across the pastures. The ranch had come back to life since her high school days dating Luke. Back then it had had a desperate sort of taint, like fabric fraying around the edges. A once-prosperous ranch sliding down in decline despite the desperate efforts of Luke's father to hold it together.

Now, the ranch gave off the air of new life, of the fresh start Luke's brother, Gunner, had launched after taking over a few years earlier. The place struck her as both familiar and different.

And soaked in too many memories.

This guy's meaner than the bulls he used to ride, one note from the therapist at the other agency had said. *I'm not going back there. Let someone in Austin have at him.*

I can't handle him, another note complained. *I say let this cowboy recover on someone else's watch.*

It had been such a huge blessing when Ruby's clinical instructor and mentor, Lana Donmeyer, chose to make Ruby a partner in her practice and allow Ruby to open a satellite facility here in Martins Gap. Even if Lana called Ruby "bright and gifted," to land this type of semi-partnership setup fresh out of school was practically unheard of. Dad's life insurance money was supposed to be for Mama, not funding a fledgling practice. She'd pay Mama back, even if Mama said her staying close in Martins Gap to help with Grandpa was payment enough.

Luke Buckton could be a landmark patient for her. As a high profile rider, with a high profile injury, getting Luke back on his feet could really launch her career. Even Lana said so. Yes, there was *so much* history between them. But today was her chance to show that cowboy what she was made of now that six years had gone by.

She'd been full of resolve...until she pulled up to the big house. The sight of the place quickly dissolved into a blur of memories that overthrew her control.

She'd been so happy here.

She'd been so miserable here.

A quick look around as she got out of the car revealed no one but "Granny B" standing on the house's big porch. Ruby found herself telling her limbs to get out of the car.

"Ruby," came Adele Buckton's warm voice as she hobbled down off the porch. "My stars, but it's Ruby Sheldon."

"Hi, Granny B." The words belonged to some eighteen-year-old version of herself, young and squeaky. It wasn't as if they hadn't crossed paths over the years, small as Martins Gap was, but neither of them could pretend this was anything but awkward and difficult.

"Look at you." Her gaze fell to the folder in Ruby's hand. "You're here for Luke." Somehow Granny B made the simple statement sound as complex as it truly was.

"Yes, ma'am." She wished for something more clever to say, but came up short.

Ruby had always liked Granny B—the Buckton children all called her "Gran" but everyone else in town called her "Miss Adele" or "Granny B." The old woman had been as much of an anchor as Luke ever had in high school. Luke and his dad locked horns on a near constant basis, and Luke's mom had passed when he was eleven. Though he had three siblings—including a twin—they'd all pretty much been born with one foot out the door. Granny B had been the one responsible for anything that felt homey and welcoming about this place.

When Luke left town after graduation, Ruby had wanted—expected, actually—for Granny B to show up and make sense of how Luke broke things off. She'd always been so sure either Granny B or Luke's twin sister, Tess, would appear on her doorstep and explain why the boy she loved both left her and left Martins Gap without a backward glance. It had never happened.

Granny B's gaze lifted over Ruby's head to settle on the guesthouse behind them. Ruby turned to see the guesthouse door open up. The figure of Luke Buckton stood in half shadow behind the screen door.

"I'd best leave you to it, then," Gran was saying behind her.

Ruby's heart twisted and surged and stung all at the same time. A hollowed-out panic, an empty awareness froze her chest—all feelings that made no sense but surrounded her anyway as she stared at him.

He was just like the ranch—familiar yet different. The eyes were still their spellbinding blue—"Buckton blue," everybody called it—but now they were framed by tight features. His wild-boy hair still tumbled around that strong jaw, only now the jaw was roughened with a man's stubble. Luke had filled out into a man's body, lean and hard-edged, but even his defiant stance didn't quite conceal the hint of uncertainty that made him favor one leg. How he could be the boy of her memory and a stranger before her at the same time made Ruby's mind spin.

"Ruby." His voice, somehow octaves deeper now, held more challenge than welcome. "Why are you here?"

It was an absurd question—they both knew why she was here. His prickly tone held the faintest hint of the dismissive words he'd flung at her the night he told her he was leaving. Not just Martins Gap, but her as well.

The tone snapped something to life in her, resurrecting all the anger against him she'd swallowed down over the years. It was helpful—clearing her head and straightening her spine, giving her the composure to calmly call his bluff. "You need help."

Need and *help* weren't in Luke Buckton's vocabulary back then, and she doubted he was friendly with the concepts now.

She'd read the file. No one really knew what level of functionality Luke Buckton would get back from his left leg. Such injuries were unpredictable.

"Well, now, that's a matter of opinion," Luke replied as he flexed one hand against the doorknob. Rather flippant for someone in his position—but then again, that tactic had been a Luke Buckton specialty.

"No," she retorted, "I'd say that's a medical fact." When she saw the edge in his eyes give just a little, she pressed further. "Whether or not you're man enough to accept it…well, I expect *that* is a matter of opinion."

She'd never have spoken like that to any other patient, but no one could call Luke Buckton "any other patient." She heard Granny B mutter something that sounded approving and the big house door shut behind her.

Luke looked at her with an almost amused disdain, as if some uppity puppy had taken to yapping at one of the thousand-pound bison that were raised on the ranch. A "don't you know who you're dealing with?" warning glare. Frustration made people hard and sour, especially those for whom weakness was an unforgivable sin. She knew that his frustration was why he'd pushed away the other therapists, and it told her he was that frightened he wouldn't heal. And yet despite their history, he hadn't tried to hire in a therapist from Austin, even when he knew Ruby was the only option left in town. Which meant that while he'd never admit to it, he'd decided he needed her.

He'd done exactly the same thing in high school when they'd met as she tutored him in algebra. That boy had gone all "I don't need you" when she was the only thing standing between him and failing out his senior year.

Begrudgingly needing her had turned into respecting her, had turned into liking her, had turned into—she'd thought—loving her. That boy had made her feel pretty and full of possibility…only to turn around months later and declare her not pretty enough and without enough potential to follow him to rodeo stardom.

She suddenly realized it had been half a minute or so, and neither of them had spoken.

Luke shifted his weight again. It dawned on Ruby that while she could wait all day for this standoff to end, he could not. He'd been injured, and badly. He may be in possession of all the bravado, but she was in possession of the solution—if there was one.

"This won't work," he said under his breath but still loud enough for her to hear. How many times had she heard those words during Luke's tirades about algebra and graduation requirements?

The remark revealed just how much he *needed* this to work. He hadn't changed: the more he needed it, the less he'd act like he did. She could see it, clear as day, because sensing things about patients was her gift.

She did have a gift. The bravest, strongest version of herself looked Luke straight in the eye. She clutched her file and took a step toward him. "Won't work, huh? Prove it."

Chapter Two

The red scarf didn't suit her.

It was a weird thought to have, given the drama of seeing the girl you'd loved and left after so much time, but that was the first thing that went through his mind.

Ruby, despite her name, wasn't a red girl. She was more of a dusky pink, the color of Gran's roses that ran along the back of the house. Red was trying too hard.

The Ruby of his memory was a soft pink thing, kitten-like, full of wonder and amazed at whatever he did. She'd put him on a mile-high pedestal all through high school, and he'd liked that. Dad was lightning-quick with the put-downs, but Ruby looked at him—as Gran would put it—as if he hung the moon.

He'd given her plenty of reason to admire him when they'd gotten to know each other.

He'd swept her off her feet. First by accident, just to distract her from the tutoring she was supposed to be giving him, and then on purpose. The more he got to know her, the more he liked her. He'd delighted in romancing her with dramatic gestures and flat-out charm. By the spring of their senior year, *like* had turned to *love*.

And then he'd done her wrong. Dropped her as dramatically and abruptly as he'd swept her up. If he could manage to regret anything—which was a reach for the likes of him—what he'd done to Ruby would top the list.

Which made today excruciating on any number of levels.

Right at this moment, however, what topped his list was that he couldn't stand up much longer. The numbness was creeping up his leg, his sense of the floor beneath his left foot all but gone. If he turned to walk back into the house now, there was a fair chance his foot would drag against the ground, if not trip him outright. He'd left his cane back at the couch, determined to stand there on his own two feet and show her he was still strong. Now the only thing that felt strong was the throbbing in his wrist from the choke hold he currently had on the doorknob.

This was the part he hated the most—he couldn't tell if his knee would hold him or buckle, if his ankle would bend or drag. It was as if his body had dismembered itself, splitting off into strange pieces that refused to talk to each other.

It'd be so much easier if it just hurt, just as it would be so much simpler if it didn't have to be Ruby.

As it was, she walked up to the guesthouse and stood waiting for an invitation to enter. The Ruby he'd known would have gotten back into her car after his first mean glare. This Ruby who'd just said "prove it" was an older, harder Ruby. It bugged him that he might be the reason for some of that armor.

"Are you going to let me in?" Her voice tried too hard to be loud, mismatched to her personality just like the scarf the wind kept flapping up off her neck.

"Do I have to?" The comeback sounded childish. Stupid, given that getting her here was what he'd wanted in the first place. He'd thought she was the only one who could get him out of this. Now that she stood in front of him, most of him hated the idea.

Ruby stared at him, one eyebrow scrunched down in thought—the way she used to stare at a math problem. It had been one of his favorite things, watching Ruby's mind whir into gear, but the fact that she was now trying to solve *him* sent an itchy feeling down his spine.

"I forgot something in the car," she said. It had the tone of a convenient excuse, and Luke swallowed the infuriating sense that she recognized his dilemma and was giving him a chance to spare his pride.

Ruby made an exaggerated turn back toward her car. Luke wasn't foolish enough to ignore the out she gave him and hobbled awkwardly back to the couch while she had her back turned. He left the door open. He couldn't decide if he should be glad she'd given him the chance to sit down unseen, or ticked off she'd sensed he needed it. That was always the best and worst thing about Ruby— she could read him like a book.

"You always wanted Granny B to let you live here," came her voice as she closed the guesthouse's front door behind her. There was no nostalgia in her tone; she recited it like fact, the way she'd recited the algebra theorems that gave him fits in school.

Luke let his hand lead his numb leg to come up and cross casually over his good knee. She was watching the way his leg moved, and he fought the urge to cover it with the issue of

Pro Bull Rider magazine lying on the couch next to him.

Ruby settled herself in the chair opposite him, a file and clipboard balanced on her lap. She sat upright, knees together, elbows close, the way she used to sit with him in study hall back before he'd coaxed her out of her shell. Ruby had always been a much more entertaining equation to solve than algebra.

"This won't work," he challenged again, knowing it made no sense but needing to keep her at a distance until the knots in his gut settled.

"So you said." Her eyes fell to the cane he'd forgotten to hide in his rush to get "casually" settled on the couch before she came in the door, and he bit back a scowl. She gave him what he was sure was her worst "therapist" glare. "Don't think I haven't heard that kind of talk before."

She'd heard it from *him* all those times he'd said he'd never be able to learn algebra. The history in the air between them was so thick and painful he could practically reach out and press his hand up against it like a cement wall.

Ruby opened her file folder with an infuriatingly clinical air. "Left leg, nerve root injury close to the spinal cord. Concussion, loss of consciousness at the time of injury. Ongoing symptoms include loss of muscle strength and neuropathy."

Luke despised the clinical terms they used—why couldn't they just say that a mean bull threw him against a fence at an event in Montana, knocked him out, and busted up his back. He remembered the ride, but any memory of the grisly fall came from video tape—he only woke up afterward in an ambulance with several panicked people poking and asking urgent questions.

"How would you rate your current level of pain?"

She'd have read every page of his file, so she knew that was a trick question. This new Ruby Sheldon wasn't playing nice. "Ain't nothin'," he drawled, omitting the wink he usually gave the buckle bunnies. Those pretty, love-struck rodeo fans usually cooed and pouted over his collection of bruises and scratches after a show. They'd showed up at the hospital the first two days, then trickled off as the tour moved on.

Her eyes narrowed, and she clicked her pen. "On a scale of one to ten, please." He had to admit to a shred of surprise that she could produce such a hard shell in his presence. Maybe hate really was more powerful than love, like Dad always said.

"Point-five."

"Do you have difficulty with any limbs other than the involved leg?"

He sat back against the couch cushions. "I've been told all of me works just fine."

That irritated her—those kinds of lines always did. She stood up and put her hands on her hips.

"Stand up."

He glared at her. "You know, I believe I'm fine right here."

Something shot through her eyes, a stubbornness that surprised him. "Stand up. I'm not going to be scared off, so how long this takes is entirely up to you. Let's try standing for eight seconds. That ought to be a time frame you know well."

Eight seconds. The length of a qualifying bull ride. Whenever she'd worried about how much risk or pain was involved in bull riding—which had been often—he'd always said, "Honey, I can take anything for eight seconds." He hadn't expected her to use their history against him.

Luke Buckton had burned a heap of bridges on his way out of this tiny town, and now it felt as if he was going to have to fight to keep the pile of ashes from rising up and choking him.

Ruby made herself look straight at Luke as he pulled his long body up off the couch. He was trying hard to hide every single weakness—physical and otherwise—but she wouldn't allow it. *I'm as stubborn as you are, Luke Buckton. And I have just as much riding on this as you do.* Lana was right; success with a high profile client like him would bolster business. But right now, Ruby mostly just wanted to show Luke up. *Who's stronger now, cowboy?*

She spied a straight-backed chair up against the wall and dragged it to his side. "Hold on to this and put all your weight on your good leg."

Luke shot her a look, and she suspected he was concocting some remark about all of him being more than good, but he simply grabbed the chair and rocked back on one hip as if leaning against a bar in an Old West saloon.

"Raise your left leg as far as you can and hold it there, please."

Effort tightened the corners of his cocky smile. He got the injured leg up about as far as his knees, and she noticed a tremor near the top.

"Like the boots?" He pointed toward his expensive-looking cowboy boots. Ruby guessed they cost as much as her used car. "Custom work. Gift from a sponsor."

"Very nice," she replied. "Take them off."

"What?"

"I can hardly see how your ankle rotates if you've got it locked up inside all that fine, hand-tooled leather now, can I?"

He frowned. "None of the other gals made me take off my boots."

Ruby wasn't backing down. "None of the other *therapists*," she emphasized the correction in terms, "got that far before you drove them off."

There was a long, prickly pause before he said, "I can't."

It must have cost him to say that. His bitter tone made her hair stand on edge. He looked like a porcupine, defensive spines sticking out in all directions, warning the world to keep its distance.

Her heart twisted at the anguish she wondered if only she could see. Luke was deeply hurting, but scrambling to keep it hidden. It gave her only one way forward: if she was going to treat him, she'd have to meet his defenses head-on.

But this was Luke. Luke with those eyes

and all that history. Ruby made herself hold his gaze despite the monster-sized flip it caused in her stomach. "You can't what?" she asked as directly as she knew how. *Do not back down.*

He stared at her for a long moment. "I can't get 'em on and off without…help."

The last word stuck, as if he'd had to drag it up from some pit to say it out loud.

Cowboys pulled their boots off every day. Most did it without even thinking, either heel-to-toe or with a fancy little hook-like gizmo set up beside many Texan doorways. Way back, she'd seen Luke do it hundreds of times. Of course, such maneuvers required standing on one leg—something Ruby was pretty sure Luke could no longer do.

Ruby carefully turned the straight chair so that the seat faced forward. If getting him to receive help came in the form of this near standoff just to remove his boots, then this was as good a place as any to start.

Grace. Was she strong enough to extend grace to the man who had hurt her so deeply back then? The moment suddenly struck her as equally important to her as it was to him. If she claimed to come as far as she had from the teenager Luke had left behind, the proof would come in what she did next.

Slowly, Ruby kneeled down at the foot of the chair and motioned for Luke to sit. "Well, then, help it is."

The gesture startled him—she watched the astonishment flash across his features before he hid them behind that famous grin. A deep resolve settled into place under her breastbone, the same resolve that had gotten her through all her therapist schooling with record speed and exemplary grades despite a mountain of obstacles.

She folded her hands in her lap and stared up at him. *I'll sit here for an hour if that's what it takes, Luke. I expect you know that. I expect that's why I'm here. So come on, cowboy, what's it gonna be?*

The long, tall body still held an athlete's lines. The take-on-the-world planes of his shoulders, the try-and-stop-me set of his jaw. And yet, despite his strength and determination, all his features seemed to tip on the knife's edge of a man in doubt. Ruby found herself doing what she'd never thought she'd do again: praying for Luke Buckton.

Slowly—excruciatingly slowly and with all the ferocity of a bull fixing to charge—Luke sat down.

Chapter Three

Ruby drove a bit down the road before she eased her little car to the shoulder. She let out the breath she'd been holding since pulling the guesthouse door shut behind her and allowed her head to sink against the steering wheel.

The longest hour of my life.

Once Luke sat down, Ruby had expected things to smooth out. Having broken down the barrier and earned that one shred of compliance, she'd expected to gain more.

She'd forgotten who she was dealing with.

Oh, she'd gotten the boot off all right—albeit with a comical sequence of yanks and tugs—to expose the injured foot. When she asked him to use that foot, to show her his range of motion with the ankle or anything else, Luke turned mean. His frustration nearly darkened the room, it was so intense.

Luke had always had a temper—it was probably half of what made him such a good rider. Something came over him when he got angry, a laser-sharp focus and determination that plowed through anything standing in his way. He'd spent most of his teenage years angry, primarily at his father, and that anger had driven him not just to succeed but to excel. Now that anger was directed at his own body, which made it much more vicious as it spilled out onto anyone foolish enough to be in range. *Lord*, Ruby sent up a moan of a prayer, *he's a wounded animal—twice as mean and four times as dangerous.*

It wasn't as if Ruby didn't know how to handle an ornery patient. Difficult patients were, in fact, a specialty of hers. Lana said, "Your greatest talent is seeing through the hard actions to the wounded soul beneath." When Lana grafted Ruby into her agency, setting up Martins Gap Physical Therapy as an affiliated partnership of Lana's own practice in Austin, she'd said it was because of Ruby's gifts. "You always find the one gesture that will open up a crack in the walls patients build around themselves." Ruby could always find a crack and pry it open.

Today that gift felt more like a curse. The true torment of the last hour wasn't Luke's behavior—that was just a coping mechanism, the battle weapon of a man at the end of his rope.

No, her real problem was her ability to see through him. To peer under the gleam of the brilliant shell he showed the world and see a man who wasn't sure he could pull off the recovery he needed. A massive cauldron of doubt and pain boiled under that cocky disregard. She'd seen it for just a moment as he sat down, but within minutes of that glimpse he'd slammed the shell back on with the ferocity of the bull bison who wandered the Blue Thorn pastures.

Ruby's cell phone buzzed beside her, and she fished it from her handbag to peer at the screen.

Been praying for you. Call me when it's over.

Lana was the best instructor and mentor Ruby could ever ask for. Mama and Grandpa were supportive, but Lana often knew just how to bolster her spirits. It was probably due to Lana's prayers that Ruby had lasted as long as she had with Luke.

Forgoing a text, Ruby dialed her mentor,

taking a deep breath as Lana clicked on the line before the first ring even finished.

"And how was the Buckton beast?"

"Beastly," she replied, glad to feel a damp laugh bubble up from all the tension in her chest.

"Does he look like you remember?"

"Oh, his looks have improved with age. Those eyes are still…those eyes. I'd forgotten how dark they could turn. That man's angry glare could set a tree on fire."

"That charming, huh?"

"Let's just say I'm not so sure the Blue Thorn bulls have the worst temper on that ranch. If he's the charmer of the bull riding circuit, I didn't see any of it."

"A mean son of gun, hmm?"

Ruby let her head fall back against the seat rest. "He was mean—but not in the way you might think. He didn't yell at me or call me names. His methods were more cold. Heartless. Wisecracking and dismissive."

"Ouch. How are you?"

Ruby looked back at the Blue Thorn's rolling pastures that filled her rearview mirror. "I don't know. I mean, I knew it'd be hard. But it was so much harder than hard—if that makes any sense. It felt more like sixty hours than sixty minutes."

"Did you get him to do anything?"

In fact, she had. That was the one foothold she had in this mess, and no one could grab hold of an ounce of progress better than Ruby Sheldon. "Two exercises. And I tricked him into showing me his range of motion, which isn't much at all. He thinks he'll be back on a bull, that's clear."

"Will he? What sense do you get about his prognosis?"

"I have no way of knowing. At least not yet. If anybody could pull it off though, it'd be him."

"Only…" Lana had caught the hesitation in her voice.

Ruby let one hand rest on the file. She'd have to write down her notes from the visit, and that would feel so very odd. It'd be a challenge to think of Luke Buckton in purely clinical terms. "You know how this goes. It may not be up to him."

"Do you feel like it's up to you?"

"No. Yes. Honestly, I don't know. Even the best therapy program we have, followed to the letter, can only do so much." Lana was the seasoned professional, but Ruby had seen patients throw themselves wholeheartedly into therapy and then progress both more and less than anyone expected—and it wasn't always clear why. "I suppose it's up to God more than anything else."

She could hear Lana sigh on her end. She'd told her mentor the entire history she and Luke had together. "Ruby, I know I told you he could be a high-profile client for you, but is it worth it? You don't owe this man anything. I'm sure he could pay anybody to come from Austin and take his bad attitude three times a week for thirty minutes."

"I'm not so sure he can, Lana."

"Don't those guys earn big bucks? I read the guy who won last year's championships was worth millions."

"In the big series, yes. Luke's not quite there yet. Besides, you don't earn if you can't ride, and Luke's been out of commission since June. His sponsors may have all pulled out already. I don't think he'd be back on the Blue Thorn unless it was his only option. Luke wasn't coming home until he came home a champion, you know?"

"Don't start making excuses for him. You told me you spent months crying over that man."

Ruby closed her eyes. "I did. But I'm not that girl anymore, either."

"And you just proved that. You could walk

away from this right now and I would back you up."

"I don't quit on patients."

"Luke Buckton isn't 'a patient.' He's an emotional minefield. Hearing the way you sound right now, I'm sorry I ever encouraged you to take him on. This can't end well—for you or for him. You've got way too much water under the bridge."

Lana was right. Their history did make things worse. "I know, Lana, but maybe it's time to burn that bridge. After all, if I can get through Luke Buckton's treatment, then I'll know for sure I'll never quit on a patient."

"All right, I told myself I wasn't going to ask this, but I have to know. You don't still carry a torch for him, do you?"

The most startling thing about today had been the tiny, irrational part of her that *did* still care. The flicker of against-her-will compassion that made her walk to the car for a "forgotten" file just to save his dignity. It stunned her how, after all the ways he'd hurt her, her heart could resurrect any care at all.

"He needs grace." It was true, but even she knew it wasn't the whole truth.

"Perhaps," Lana sighed. "But maybe it doesn't need to come from you."

Ruby looked back at the ranch in her rearview mirror. "Maybe I need to know I'm strong enough to show him grace. Maybe I need the closure I never got. Maybe I want the chance to walk away from Luke in a way that showed more mercy than the way he walked away from me."

"I just want to be sure you're taking him on for the right reasons. Professional concern isn't the same thing as nostalgic sympathy."

Sympathy was the last thing Luke wanted, or needed. That man needed someone to wage war on his condition, maybe even to wage war on the man himself.

If Ruby Sheldon was anything, she was a warrior.

Luke eased himself up off the hay bale as he watched his brother, Gunner, check some records in the barn after lunch. Nobody had yet said a word about Ruby's visit—not even Gran, who he'd expected to cross the lawn the minute Ruby's car was out of sight and grill him for details.

Lunch was an excruciating exercise in avoiding the topic. Gran, Gunner, Gunner's wife of two years, Brooke, Brooke's ten-year-old daughter, Audie, and even their seven-month-old boy, Trey, seemed to stare holes in him while talking about every other subject they could find. Good. Everyone ought to know the subject of Ruby Sheldon was off-limits. Still, Luke wondered how long that reprieve would last.

He balanced his weight on the good leg until he knew how well the bad one was working at the moment—an annoyingly necessary tactic these days—and leaned up against the barn wall as casually as possible. It was always an endless negotiation to be upright. How long would it be before he threw his leg over the back of a motorcycle without a second thought again? Over the back of a horse? A bull? He'd pressed both his surgeons in Montana, as well as the specialist he'd seen in Austin, but no one had any timelines to give.

Go ahead, ask me. Gunner could never leave well enough alone where he was involved, and after Ruby's visit Luke was itching for a fight anyhow. He'd thought he'd appreciate the quiet of the ranch, but the truth was the inactivity was making him nuts. The guesthouse—the whole ranch—was too quiet, too slow, too watchful. One of his motorcycles was still in the ranch garage, and if he thought he stood half a chance of driving it with any control, he'd be off down the road in a heartbeat.

Gunner looked up to catch Luke's stare. "I suppose it's none of my business," his brother said, replying to the question Luke hadn't asked.

"It isn't. But you're gonna ask anyway, so go ahead."

"Why are you being such an idiot?"

Luke was expecting a more specific question, but wasn't it just like Gunner to paint his entire life in idiotic terms instead of just his attitude toward Ruby? It stumped him for a reply—Luke wasn't sure where to start.

Gunner, evidently, knew exactly where to start. He straightened up, making Luke resent every one of the three inches Gunner had on him. "I thought Ruby showed a lot of spine coming out here after the way you've been behaving. Tell me, is it all an act, or are you really just that mean now?"

"I can't stand any of that stupid 'stretch this way' and 'push against here' nonsense."

Gunner returned his gaze to the papers. "So you've got this all figured out then. You'll just heal on your own and be back to break new bones next season." Gunner looked so much like their father it made Luke want to kick something. As if he could. It had been so hard to get his boot back on after Ruby left that the frustration was eating him alive.

"It's worked before." Luke crossed his arms over his chest. "Come on, this isn't the first time I've come up hurt." It wasn't. But it was the first time he had come up hurt *this bad*.

"No," Gunner replied as he closed the ledger and shoved it back into a drawer. "But forgive me for pointing out this is the first time you've come *home*."

Luke's teeth ground at Gunner's words. That was just like his big brother to cut right to the marrow without mercy. Luke fished for a good comeback, and came up empty. Instead he found a nail in the wall beside him and began to wiggle it loose.

"I know you." Gunner went on. "I've *been* you. You wouldn't be here if it weren't your last chance."

"This is not my last chance," Luke shot back as he yanked the nail from the wall. He glared at Gunner's lousy, end-of-the-road choice of words. "I figured it was time to show up, that's all."

"That's a load of bull, and you know it." Gunner met his glare with one of his own. "How about you just stop pretending this isn't a major setback?"

"It's not a major setback." Now he was really starting to sound like a five-year-old. *Go ahead, Gunner, don't hold back. Go for 'career-ending' why don't you? You won't be the first, and right now I'd love a reason to punch you.* He threw the nail into a nearby barrel and found another one to work loose.

Gunner grabbed his hand on the nail and gripped it tight to hold it still. "Don't you get it, Luke? No one here cares whether or not you ride next season. Whether you win the tour next season or world championship the season after that or never get on a bull again. This is your family. You don't have to go all 'big shot' on us. You surely didn't have to go all 'big shot' on Ruby or anyone else."

"Nobody needs to baby me!" Luke yanked his hand out from under Gunner's, the nail underneath leaving a small scrape on his palm. He shook his hand and then sucked on the wound while turning to head out the barn door. Every inch of him wanted to storm out, but his slow gait made it impossible.

"More bull. You're hurt. Bad, if I had to guess—and I *have* to guess, don't I? Because you're not saying anything." Gunner walked up and stood right in front of him now, his softened expression even worse than his previous glare. "Luke," he said, in lower tones, glancing back toward the big house as if keeping his words away from prying ears, "just how bad are you hurt? Really?"

"Nothin' to tell," Luke dodged, shrugging.

"I don't buy that for a minute. Talk to me. It's eating you alive, man, even I can see it."

His brother's words started up a war in Luke's chest—the need to talk waging battle with the need to keep everyone from knowing. His surgeons and even the local doc had been sworn to secrecy. His agent didn't know the whole of it. If even a hint of this ever made it back to his sponsors...

"Don't know," he said finally, feeling rattled by even letting that much slip out.

"Of course you know."

"No, I mean I really don't know. Nobody does. It's not pain. I'd be better if it were just pain. It's..." He'd kept it bottled up for long enough that it fairly boiled inside him, desperate to get out. "I don't feel *anything*. The nerves—they're shot. At least for now. And nobody knows if they'll stay that way."

Gunner was wrong. It didn't help to tell someone. It felt as if saying it aloud let the facts take root in the real world instead of just infesting his worries. The weight of not knowing felt heavier than ever.

Luke took a step toward his brother, hating how much effort the action involved. "So all the stupid therapies in the world can't change the fact that I may have fried my leg, get it?"

He hissed the words like the threat they were. "Either the feeling's coming back or it ain't. I've got no say in how this ends. None." He jabbed an angry finger at Gunner and his infuriatingly compassionate expression. "So forgive me if I'm not a ball of sunshine about the whole thing. I need to beat this. I need to get my leg back. I need to show the whole tour that I am not washed-out for good."

"Luke…"

"Don't!" Luke shot back. "Don't you dare give me that 'don't give up hope look.' I can't take that from you. Or from Ruby, or from anybody." He started making his way back to the guesthouse, needing to get out of the open space where anybody could watch him limp. A thought turned him around—*why did it always take so much effort to turn around?*— and he gave Gunner the darkest look he could manage. "Not one word to Gran. Or Ellie. Or anyone. Understand?"

Gunner held up his hands. "I get it. They ought to know, but if you don't want…"

"Not one word," Luke repeated, turning back toward the house.

Gunner's voice came after him. "Ruby knows. She's got your file, so she knows, doesn't she?"

Luke just kept walking.

Chapter Four

"You came back."

Ruby couldn't read the look on Luke's face Wednesday morning as he opened the guesthouse door. Was he surprised, pleased or irritated? Likely all of the above, she decided. "Yes, I am. Surprised?"

At least he'd met her at the door, not just left it open as if she were some stray animal allowed to wander in. It was easier this time—she'd survived the initial shock of seeing him. She'd always wondered what it would feel like to see him again, and now she knew. He had less power over her composure now. Oh, he could still set her stomach tumbling with one look—a gal would have to be dead not to feel something when those brilliant blues met hers—but the tumble was something other than attraction now. Nostalgia? Regret? Pity?

Whatever it was, Ruby knew it wasn't anger. Determination, maybe, but not anger. "Clock's a' ticking, cowboy. Are you going to let me in or are we going to chitchat in your doorway?"

Luke scratched his chin. "Yes, ma'am." Clearly he wasn't expecting the "all business" version of Ruby today. He gestured her inside, but stood where he was so she had to sidestep close to him to gain entrance. *Classic Luke*, Ruby thought as she set down her bag. *Always going for the swoon.*

Well, today *was* business. She pointed to Luke's sneakers. "I see you took my suggestion." She'd shown him grace and compassion on her last visit, because he deserved it. He'd admitted a weakness to her in the business about the boots, and she knew how hard that was for him. Today, she'd make him work, and she hoped her request for athletic footwear gave him a hint of what to expect.

"I do know how to cooperate," he teased, flashing a smile.

"Is that so? Give me thirty minutes before I agree, will you?" She found the chair he'd sat on last week and moved it to the center of the floor. "Have a seat."

Last time, it had taken Luke almost a full minute to acquiesce and sit down. Ruby had no intention of letting it turn into a battle of wills this time. Instead, she dropped her bag to the floor as if this were no big deal, sat down at the foot of the chair the way she had before, and began pulling equipment out of her bag. She didn't even look up at Luke. Instead, she adopted an air of expected compliance, fiddling and arranging her equipment until he settled himself uneasily in the chair in front of her. *See now, that wasn't so hard for either of us.*

Ruby positioned his feet. "Raise your toes, one foot at a time."

He scoffed. "I figured we'd start with something a bit harder than toe touches."

"Ankle flexing," she corrected, "and you'll get the hard stuff when you've earned it. Plus, you have to answer questions while you do them." She placed her hand a few inches above Luke's feet, giving him a target. He easily tapped her palm with his right toes, but struggled to hit her palm with his left. "Any tingling or burning sensations in the morning?"

"No," he replied. "Are you married?"

Startled, she looked up at him. "What?"

"You get a question, so I get a question. Fair's fair."

Ruby sat back. "That's not how this goes." She returned her hand to above his feet. "Again, please, five times each."

Luke began the exercises, but launched a running commentary as he did so. "I'm guessing no, on account of I'd probably have heard about it if you were. And your name's still Sheldon."

"Lots of women keep their names when they marry these days, Luke." She noticed his left foot was raising lower and lower with each attempt. Numbness aside, Luke had lost a lot of muscle strength.

"Maybe, but not you. You'd be Mrs. Who-ever. So there is no Mr. Whoever, is there?"

Ruby grabbed Luke's ankles and gently tugged them toward her. It was time to let Luke know she wasn't putting up with any antics. She could throw him off balance— literally—anytime she chose to do so.

"Whoa," he yelped as he gripped the chair to keep upright. "A little warning, if you don't mind."

"A little courtesy, if you don't mind. Toes in and out, making a V, ten times. Count them out, so you won't be tempted to flap your jaw."

With just a touch of repentant rascal in his

eyes, Luke complied. When he finished, she offered, "I'm single. And fine with it, I might add, not that you'd understand."

"Hey, I'm single too, you know."

"Single with a long line of buckle bunnies trailing after you, which isn't the same thing." Ruby moved to kneel beside his good leg. "Raise your foot out in front of you, knee-high, ten times," and when he opened his mouth to make some smart-aleck comeback she added, "Counting out loud."

Luke settled back in his chair, giving her a look Ruby presumed Gran was sick of by now. "One…two…I'm generous with my time to fans…three…four…no harm in that."

"So I've heard. Not that I follow your career closely." She had tried to keep from following Luke's career at all, but in Martins Gap that was easier said than done. People never spoke directly to her about it, given their history, but it wasn't hard to see a clipping posted on the bulletin board at Lolly's Diner or hear neighbors boast at Shorty's Pizza. The whole church had prayed for him when word of the accident hit town.

"Eight…I got enough get-well cards… nine…to wallpaper the guesthouse three times over." While that had the air of exaggeration she'd expect from Luke Buckton, she didn't doubt that the cards had poured in after his injury. Even Ruby knew, however, that the "Will Buckton return?" speculation in sports media had dropped off the minute the battle between the next two tour contenders heated up. The spotlight lost no time in moving on, and a man like Luke thrived on attention. What happened when you took that away at his most vulnerable moment?

"Now the other leg, only five on this one."

Luke couldn't go as high as his good leg, but he dug in and raised it ten times to match the other instead of the five she'd assigned. "That stubborn streak of yours will serve you well, but when I say five, I mean five. Not ten. You can't overdo this if you want those nerves to wake up."

"*When* those nerves wake up."

Ruby wasn't in the business of lying to patients, even with the kindest of lies. "*If* those nerves wake up." When he glared at her, she added, "So let's do our best to make sure they do."

He was quiet for the next exercise, and downright silent when his leg refused to comply for the following one.

"So have there been any potential Mr. Whoevers?" he leaned in and asked.

Ruby knew a diversion when she saw one. She shifted to a less taxing exercise and said, "As a matter of fact, there have. Not that I'd name names with the likes of you."

"Gran told me you dated an insurance salesman from Waco for a time. An insurance salesman." He coated the last three words with generous disdain.

Ruby slapped her file shut. "If you already knew the details of my social life, why'd you ask?" She pointed to his leg, an unspoken command to do the current exercise again.

"I wanted to hear it from you."

"You wanted to gloat over my small-town choice of beaus, you mean."

He grinned. "Well, that, too."

"Okay then, let's hear about your relationships. The serious ones. Lasting more than two nights or one town."

Luke stretched his leg toward her extended hand, his voice tightening with the effort. "Don't do those."

"You mean don't do those *anymore*." The jab left her mouth before she could catch it back. He'd been "serious" with her and they both knew it.

It stopped Luke in his tracks, his leg dropping to the floor. "I suppose I deserved that," he said after a long pause. "So we're gonna talk about it, then?"

"No," Ruby shot back.

Should they talk about it? Luke knew full well the danger of opening up that can of worms. He'd loved her—as much as a seventeen-year-old boy could love anyone. He'd bucked all the put-downs from the other guys on the football team about dating "the brainiac" instead of this year's collection of cheerleaders.

If he and Ruby started talking about it, he'd wind up needing to apologize, and he wasn't ready for that. Of course, he knew he'd broken her heart. But he didn't believe he'd made the wrong decision. She wasn't rodeo material. Even if he had taken her with him, the circuit would have eaten her alive. The press liked him much better with a rotation of pretty things hanging on each arm. According to Nolan Riggs, his agent, Luke's good looks were an asset, and "…and he's single, ladies!" was as much a part of his marketing as how much the camera loved his Buckton-blue eyes.

"Okay," he said as he took the small plastic ball she'd told him to roll under his bad foot, "so we're not gonna talk about it. Check."

"Can you do that?" she asked. "Can you be decent and professional about this? Because if you can't, we're done right now."

He searched for a safer topic. "What was college like?" He knew she'd gotten into some fancy-pants accelerated program for physical therapy that got her out in fewer years.

"I liked it. It was fun living in Austin for a while." She pulled out some brightly colored elastic bands, wiggling her fingers through them while she decided which to use. She always did that—wiggle her fingers while she was thinking. He'd forgotten how amusing he found it.

"But you didn't stay?"

She looked up at him. "I couldn't." She paused for a moment before she explained. "Dad."

How could it have slipped his mind that her father had died when they were a few years out of high school? Gran had told him. He'd sent a card or something, hadn't he? His schedule hadn't allowed for anything like traveling home for a friend's dad's funeral. Especially when he'd been certain she wouldn't want him anywhere near her. "I knew about that. Sorry. Really."

She and her dad had been close. He remembered that. He'd been envious of it, as a matter of fact, given how bad things were between himself and his own father. Ruby simply nodded, and he watched her tuck her grief down inside a professional demeanor. She took back the little ball and looped a blue band around his outstretched feet. "Pull your knees apart from each other, slowly, ten times."

He did as she requested. It wasn't the time for some wisecrack; obviously her dad was still a tender topic. "How's your mom? Your grandpa?"

She relaxed somewhat. "Grandpa's had a rough year. He lives with Mama now. I help out as much as I can. It's why I'm so thankful to have the practice here, where I can be nearby."

He hadn't ever figured her for the kind to strike out on her own. "How'd you open your own practice?"

Ruby spoke as he went through the exercise. "My course instructor, Lana, used to work for a firm down in Austin. When it got bought out by one of the bigger firms—that happens a lot these days—she got tired of the atmosphere and offered to set up a partnership with me."

He hadn't seen this Lana nor had anyone referred him to her. "Is she here in Martins Gap now?"

"Of course not. She's got her own clientele back in Austin. I'm the satellite office. But she comes out once a week." Ruby looked up, a peculiar squint to her eyes. "We collaborate on our more difficult patients."

"So I'll meet her, then." It pleased the rascal side of him to be thought of as a "more difficult patient."

"Not if I can help it." She slipped the band off his knees and motioned for him to go back to the silly toe touches. "I owe Lana a great deal. I'd like to spare her your particular brand of charm if possible."

Luke stared at her. This new Ruby had a spine he'd never seen before. Soft as a kitten? Not Ruby Sheldon. Not anymore. As a matter of fact, he couldn't entirely say this cat didn't have claws. Maybe it *was* better if they didn't talk about their past.

"You like what you do? I mean, you can make a living at it, even out here?"

"I get a lot of hours at the medical center, and I do some home health care for seniors like Grandpa to fill in the gaps. I'm not rich like some rodeo stars," she grasped his foot and pushed it toward him, stretching out the tendon. "But I do okay. Between the two of us—Lana in Austin and me out here—we're able make it work. I had Dad's life insurance policy to help me get set up. Mama figured Dad would have wanted it that way. 'Course, that was before Grandpa got really sick."

"I'm not rolling in dough, just in case you were wondering." He didn't know why he said that. "Not yet, that is."

Ruby stopped moving his foot. "I figured. You wouldn't be here if you had any other options."

Ouch. "I have options. I just wanted some quiet."

That made her laugh. "I have never known you to crave quiet in your entire life."

"Well, maybe I've changed since we…" He'd started a sentence that wasn't safe to finish.

"I certainly hope you've changed since you left me behind." She gave the last three words a bitter edge.

Double ouch. "So I guess we *are* gonna talk about it."

"No." She pushed against his foot, harder this time, and he waited—in vain—for it to hurt. "We're not."

Chapter Five

Luke sat in his pickup in the Red Boots BBQ parking lot and watched for Ruby's dinky little car to come up the road. They'd been through two more therapy sessions—very boring, tedious therapy session where she always seemed to know if he overdid his exercises. He was glad she gave him the Fourth of July weekend off, but even now he was itching to do something other than "push, pull, stretch, bend and balance" with her.

When he'd left the phone message, he wasn't quite sure she'd agree to meet him for lunch. Red Boots was a bit out of town, but the food was good and he wasn't really ready to be seen in Martins Gap with all its peering eyes. He stood a good chance of being recognized even here, but it was the best option he could think of when Nolan called Friday and said he was coming into town today.

So now you're too chicken to meet your agent by yourself? Luke shifted in his seat, fidgety with the unfamiliar anxiety. The old Luke Buckton was fearless, and he hated this new, nervous side of him.

You want her opinion, he corrected himself. *You need her cooperation for your plan. If she hears it from Nolan, she'll take to it easier.*

Luke checked his watch. 11:25 a.m. Ruby was never late for anything. Luke, on the other hand, was always late for everything. Her eyes would pop out of her head to see him here a full five minutes ahead of time. *Yeah, well lots of things about me have changed*, he laughed to himself. He'd told Nolan to show up at noon so he'd have a chance to give Ruby a heads-up on the whole deal.

And to head Nolan off at the pass if Ruby threw a fit, which was a distinct possibility given what he was about to propose. *Time for a bit of that fearlessness, cowboy.*

Luke got out of his truck just as the sign in the Red Boots window flickered on to Open and Ruby's car swerved into the parking lot.

She looked him up and down as he walked over to her. He'd dressed sharp today, wanting to look on top of his game. If he didn't feel it, at least he could look it.

"No cane?" she asked, one eyebrow raised.

"Flying solo today. Long as you don't ask to hit the dance floor, I'll be fine." Luke gestured toward the entrance.

"But you're staying out of the hometown spotlight?" she replied as she began walking toward the door, a giant red wooden slab below a neon sign of a kicking boot. The establishment was about twenty minutes outside of Martins Gap.

"I like their food here." He kept his voice casual as he picked his way across the gravel parking lot with care.

"You like how far out of Martins Gap that food is." That was Ruby. It was always impossible to get anything past her.

"I wasn't sure you'd come," he admitted as he grabbed the big handle and heaved the heavy door open for her. The action required more effort than he remembered. If his old weight set was still in the ranch house basement, he ought to set it up in the guesthouse. The therapy was only focusing on his legs— he shouldn't let the rest of his body lose its training. "This isn't exactly standard treatment protocol."

"Getting you up and out of the house is a

good thing. And I get not wanting to do it in front of an audience." She paused for a moment before adding, "But I did think about it before I called you back, if you want to know the truth."

That was Ruby—thoughtful to his impulsiveness. Dependable in all the ways he wasn't. Mostly invisible compared to his relentless "look at me." He told himself Nolan had been right all those years ago—she never would have been happy on the tour. "I want us to be friends," he ventured, meaning it but understanding the surprised look it drew from her. "Think we can do that?"

She narrowed one eye at him, that analytical look that always used to bug him so. "I don't know."

"But you're here." That had to count for something.

"Am I here as your therapist, your friend or the girl you used to date in high school?"

She wasn't the girl he used to date in high school anymore. She was older, tougher, probably wiser, but also a bit of something else he couldn't quite put a name to just yet. He'd be lying if he said that last part didn't make him curious. "The first two." Luke stuffed one hand in his pocket as he took off his hat, unsure if that was the right answer.

"Table for three, please," he said to the girl who greeted them.

"Three?" Ruby didn't look pleased at the surprise.

"My agent's coming later to talk over something. I want to hear what you think—as a therapist and a friend—before I say yes."

She stopped following the server to glare at him. "No games, Luke."

"No games. I want Nolan to hear what you have to say and I want you to hear what Nolan has to say." He pulled the chair out for her at the table. "Straight up and simple."

She sat down, a wary look on her face. "You don't do straight up and simple."

"Let's just say I'm trying a new tactic these days." He sat himself down, grateful he didn't have to maneuver his leg into a booth. Getting in wasn't so bad, but getting out could prove a gangly hassle he wasn't ready to attempt. "I did my exercises over the holiday weekend anyway, you know."

She offered him the first smile he'd seen since arriving. "Well, this is a new Luke. I hadn't pegged you for compliance."

He grimaced. "I don't take much to that word. Willing to work at it, maybe."

"Cooperative, then."

"Easygoing," he suggested as the server brought over tall glasses of water.

"That might be pushing it. An easygoing person would have warned me I was having lunch with your agent instead of springing it on me after I'd arrived."

Luke felt himself grin. When was the last time he'd done that? There was always something about Ruby, a gift she had for putting him at ease when his ambition got the better of him.

The tour might have eaten Ruby alive, but right now he couldn't rightly say the tour hadn't eaten him alive without her. Riding a bull was a binary science: either you were on the bull, or you were off it. Either you rode, or you didn't. The clean-cut nature of that world appealed to him. It was one of the reasons all this "maybe" guesswork and "let's see how things progress" prognosis drove him crazy.

"How have things with this Nolan fellow been since the accident?"

Well, there was a loaded question. Luke fiddled with a packet of crackers from the bread basket. "Fine."

"A 'that's what I tell the public' fine or truly fine?"

"If I'm not earning, Nolan's not earning from me. Does that answer your question?"

Though the agent had a whole lineup of athletes he represented, Luke used to be one of Nolan's top clients, getting a hefty portion of the man's focused attention. Nolan used to return his phone calls within the hour. Now his phone calls got returned by the end of the day if he was fortunate. Friday's phone call had been the first one Nolan had initiated in a month. He wasn't going to share that little detail with Ruby, however. Instead, he opted for, "There's a lot riding on whether I ride."

"So Nolan wants you riding again as fast as possible, I take it?"

"Whether or not it's what Nolan wants, it's what *I* want." Luke looked around the restaurant, just starting to fill for the lunch rush. "I'm going crazy sitting around."

The server took their orders. Ruby had some safe salad thing while Luke opted for the Diablo Double super spicy BBQ sandwich. Home cooking was good, but Gran needed to learn how to use hot sauce the way it was meant to be used—generously.

"I thought you were doing your exercises. I wouldn't call that sitting around." She accepted her iced tea, and a basket of biscuits found its way to the center of the table.

"Okay, I'm standing at my kitchen counter,

marching and balancing on one leg. I'm used to a bit more excitement than that."

Ruby was quiet for a moment, and then gave Luke a direct look. "I think I'd like to hear from you first what it is Nolan is going to try to convince me to do."

"Nolan's not going to try to convince you to do anything."

"Please," she replied, giving Luke a dubious look. "Give me a bit more credit than that. You think I'll take whatever scheme is in the works more seriously if I hear it from Nolan instead of from you. Mostly because you know I'm familiar with your gift for schemes. How about you just tell me? 'Straight up' as you say."

Ruby held Luke's gaze. Clearly Luke was up to something. That man got a gleam in his eye anyone could see a mile off when he thought he was about to get away with something.

He was trying to play it straight, she thought. Ruby just wasn't sure he was capable of such a thing. Then again, he'd admitted the accident had changed him. Maybe she should give him the benefit of the doubt. It was one of the reasons she'd asked him to tell her now—she wanted to hear his version of whatever was up.

Ruby could see him decide. She was changing his game plan, and she could literally see his brain sort through the merit of her request. *You're so used to being in control,* she thought as she watched his jaw work. *How does it feel to have your future in God's hands instead of your tightfisted grasp?*

"Okay," he said slowly. She could hear his gears turning in the tone of his answer. "So you know my accident was big news."

There was an "of course" in his attitude that reminded her what a monster of an ego he had. But he also wasn't all wrong about his visibility—the photos and videos of a limp and unconscious Luke Buckton being carried from the arena had been headline footage all over Texas.

"Well, Nolan—and folks at *Pro Bull Rider* magazine, it turns out—think my recovery and comeback could be just as big news. It would also keep me in the public eye until I get back up and riding."

Ruby knew Luke saw that issue in terms of *when* and *until* and not *if,* but it struck her doubly hard right now. The fire in Luke's eyes told her the man wasn't entertaining even the slightest notion that he wouldn't return to the arena. That was a double-edged sword; determination could take a patient places medicine couldn't go, but a stubborn refusal to accept limitations could make someone overpush in a way that could be equally dangerous.

"Meaning?" She had a pretty good idea where this was going, but wanted to hear it from Luke.

"The magazine wants to do a piece on my recovery. A couple of pieces, actually. Documenting how I heal and train. If I give them exclusive access, it could be a pretty sweet deal."

Ruby pictured photographers nosing in on therapy sessions while some stunning blonde reporter hung on Luke's every word. None of it sounded like conditions she'd want to work in, much less on a case as demanding as Luke's.

"Think of it," Luke went on. "Cameras on hand to capture my first run, my first ride…"

"Your tenth fall," she cut in. "This kind of recovery doesn't go in a straight line, Luke. You're going to have setbacks. Are you sure you want an audience for that?"

"Everybody loves a comeback story. And you know me—I work best with an audience. And a finish line to strive toward."

Ruby felt her appetite leave the building. She pushed away the salad that had arrived moments earlier. "What do you have in mind for that finish line?"

"An exhibition ride."

"A ride? On *a bull*?"

"Well, not the meanest bull around, but one with—"

"Absolutely not." She started to push her chair away. "How can you even think I'd agree to something so…so…" She couldn't come up with a word for how reckless and foolhardy an idea this was.

"It's dramatic, I grant you, but I've got to—"

"No, it's not dramatic. It's irresponsible. You've been seriously hurt. We don't know the full extent of the nerve damage you've suffered, and there's no set timeline for recovery. All your publicity ideas mean that ride has to be scheduled in advance. How can you make a promise we might not be able to keep? Guarantee you'll be ready in time? You can't just cowboy up and grit your teeth past this, Luke."

"Sure I can. I'll compensate for whatever I don't have. You'll teach me."

Ruby stood up. "I can't teach you split-second reactions if you've got no sensation."

"Whoa, lower your voice," Luke hissed,

pulling her back down. "Don't say that kind of stuff where people can hear you, okay?"

Ruby made herself sit down and look him in the eye. Maybe she could get him to see reason before this doomed stunt went any further. "Don't say what's wrong with you? Don't tell you what you refuse to hear? You expect me to not only stand by and watch you potentially get yourself killed, but you want me to play guest star? Ruby Sheldon, therapist to the late, great Luke Buckton? Because trust me, Luke, that's what it'll be. You cannot do this."

"I can't just disappear, either." Luke ran a hand through his hair. "Look, Ruby, I told you how this works. No ride, no pay, no rankings. There are no sick days, no medical leave here. If the fans can't see me, they'll forget who I am. That's why this could be such a great chance. Think about it: this magazine's paying to watch me heal. What better incentive could a guy get?"

It had to be said. "And what if you don't heal? Will they want their money back?"

"I'll heal, Ruby. You know I will. You wouldn't have signed on if you didn't think I could do it."

Ruby hated that there was a grain of truth to that. Luke Buckton had made a career of beating the odds. Part of the shock of his injury came from the fact that before the incident, he'd been able to rise up from spectacular falls and ignore seemingly serious injuries. He'd once wrapped an injured arm in tape and ridden through an event only to have it leaked later that that arm had been broken in two places. If common sense ruled the day, he shouldn't even be standing up, much less contemplating an all-star comeback.

Luke leaned in. "Look me in the eye right now and tell me it's impossible. Tell me I don't stand a chance."

It was just like Luke to find the one inch of plausibility and stretch it into a mile. It was highly unlikely that he'd make a full, flawless recovery—it was foolish beyond reason to bring the media into it—but she couldn't sit there and tell him it was impossible, much as she wanted to.

"You stand a very small chance. Minute."

He leaned back, victorious. "Itty-bitty's all I need. You know that."

"But if you push yourself too hard and too fast then you stand a much larger chance of doing yourself serious harm. The you-won't-get-up-and-walk-away-from-it kind of harm. Luke, I don't see why you have to do this. And with press watching. It's not worth the risk."

"Maybe not to you."

Ruby scrambled for a way to talk him out of this before his agent came and turned it into a hopeless two-against-one. "Explain it to me, then. Make me understand why it's worth it to you to risk the rest of your life to get a spread on eight pages of a magazine."

"Ten," Luke corrected. And she wasn't really surprised when he added, "Plus the cover."

"Still not an explanation."

Luke leaned on his elbows. "I'll be twenty-five before you know it. Most guys are glad to make it to thirty and still be in the game. That means I've only got a few good years left to make my mark. How I leave sets the whole course from here as to what kind of life I'll have when I can't compete anymore—how I'll be remembered, and what position I'll be able to hold. Right now, how I left was in the back of an ambulance. I can't let that stand."

"But why choose a way back designed to kill you?"

"The whole sport's designed to kill me, Ruby. There's no 'safe' to be had, and I wouldn't want it anyway. The opportunities don't find the cowboy who limps out of the arena. I've got to go back in blazing so I can go out on top. I can't have an ordinary, safe comeback. It's all or nothing for me, always has been."

She'd heard talk like this from him before. It was part of who Luke was, what made him so good at riding. What made him able to leave her behind so he could launch his vault to stardom. The blazing comet who knew better than to try and bring the humble little pebble along for the ride.

"It's why I need you, Ruby."

The admission caught her breath.

"I can't trust anyone else to have my back while it's up against the wall like this," he went on. "You know me, you know how I work, how to get out of me what needs to come out. I've got to do this, and I know part of you understands that."

Luke was a force of nature when he got like this. He could say the craziest things, but when the drive and passion filled his eyes like they did, you couldn't help but believe crazy things were possible.

"I know what might happen. I get the risk, believe me. But if I walk away from this, it'll follow me the rest of my life. It'll all be 'what if.' I can't live like that. You know I can't."

He grabbed her hand, and she let him. The man could mesmerize without even trying.

"Look, you don't owe me anything. I know I broke your heart when I left…and I—"

"Yes, you did," she felt compelled to interject.

"And I'm sorry for that. I've got no right to ask what I'm asking, I get that. But I'm asking anyway. Help me do this. Give me this chance, no matter how crazy you think it is. You don't even have to say yes today, just listen to Nolan lay it out."

Every bone in her body, every sensible notion she possessed told her to get up and walk out. To leave Luke Buckton to his egotistical, reckless fate and have no part in what was sure to be a circus if not downright heartbreak.

"Okay."

His smile lit up the room, but it couldn't cast out every shadow that lurked in the back of her mind.

Chapter Six

"...And that's fifteen." Ruby motioned for Pastor Theo to drop the resistance band he'd been stretching with his right arm. "Do you see how much stronger you've gotten?"

"I feel it," the middle-aged pastor said. "Mostly in how much it hurts the next day." Ruby began her standard answer, but he cut in, "I know, ice and ibuprofen."

She handed him a stronger band. "You've graduated to a new color. Two more colors and you'll be swinging a golf club like that fall never happened."

He grinned. "I was hoping for *better* than when I fell."

She laughed. "I can help with strength, but your swing is up to you." Every other patient seemed so much easier than Luke these days—she hated to admit it, but the challenges of treating Luke were giving her a new appreciation for all her other work. "Arm circles are next."

Pastor Theo began moving his arms in ever-widening circles. "This is so much easier—and nicer—than driving half an hour to the medical center twice a week. I told Doc Nelson I'm much more likely to be a good patient with you right under my nose. Or me right under your thumb." He winced as his shoulder hit a tender spot. "How's it working out for you, being right here in town?"

"It's a blessing, that's for sure. I can be at Mama's at a moment's notice if I'm needed." She guided his hand through the next circle, easing up on the part that stretched his injured tendons.

"And how is your grandfather?"

Ruby sighed. "He has good days and bad days. He misses being out and about."

"I miss Gus in church. It's sad not to hear his voice from the choir loft anymore."

Grandpa's singing voice was woven through almost every childhood memory Ruby had. The rich baritone still filled the house—maybe with not quite the boom and tone it once had, but no one could sing "How Great Thou Art" like Grandpa. She'd heard the hymn probably thousands of times, and the way Grandpa sang it still gave her goose bumps.

"How much therapy would it take to get Luke Buckton to walk back through the church doors?" Theo raised an eyebrow.

Ruby waved a hand. "Now Pastor, you know I'm not supposed to talk about other patients."

"I'm not asking for your professional opinion. I wasn't here then, but I know you two have…shall we say…history. Adele's asked me to pay him a visit, and I'd like to know if you think he'd let me across his threshold. 'Cause I'd like to invite him across ours."

"Shoulder squeezes, two sets of fifteen," Ruby cued, stalling for time to think about how to answer the question of Luke's clearly lapsed faith. Had he truly lost it? Or just left it behind when he took to the circuit? "I think Luke would let you in, if only because he knew Granny B would ride him if you refused. Whether or not he'd listen, well, that's anyone's guess."

"I feel like he's at such a precarious point in his life. Who wouldn't be frightened of having to discover who you are away from the thing that defined you? If I had to suddenly stop being a pastor, I think I'd flounder for a while."

Flounder. Ruby thought of the fishing trips Grandpa used to take her on, and how the fish would flap frantically when they were pulled from the water to land on the dock. Luke showed a smooth and confident outside, but he was flapping frantically on the inside. Could everyone see that? Or just those close to him?

Was she close to him? She had been, once, but now? She needed to talk through her storm of reactions to that man, and maybe Pastor Theo was a good choice to listen.

"He's asked me to help him stage a comeback. A magazine has offered to cover his rehab and return to riding. He wants to do it."

Theo stopped mid-exercise. "Is it possible?"

"Medically speaking, there is a possibility. It's not probable, but this is Luke Buckton. I don't think the odds have ever really applied to him. Or, at least, I'm pretty sure he'll pay no attention to them."

"Have you decided to help him?" Theo's tone switched from therapist/patient to pastor/congregant.

"He says he can't do it without me. I don't know if that's how he really feels, or if that's just what he thinks will persuade me."

Theo sat back in his chair. "He doesn't

strike me as a man who listens to many people. Will he listen to you?"

"Only if I tell him what he wants to hear." Ruby closed her file. That was Theo's last exercise of the session anyway. "If he decides to push things too far—and I'm pretty sure he will, especially with press watching—I don't know that he'll listen to me or anyone if I try to rein him in."

The pastor folded his hands. "I do believe God sometimes places us next to people who need our protection. Even from themselves. It can be a wonderful thing. But it can also hurt if you don't watch yourself. What does your soul tell you? In your gut, I mean, not the therapist part."

Ruby thought about it, and then said what had kept coming to mind in the two days since her lunch at Red Boots. "I think I can help him make an effort, or at least try to make sure he doesn't kill himself in the process. Someone's got to push back against what that magazine might egg him on to do."

"Maybe that someone is you." After a moment, Theo added, "But I have to say, I don't think Luke is the only one in danger of getting hurt here. I don't know all the details, but if you were my daughter, I'd want to spare you another heartbreak at that cowboy's hands."

"Oh, there's no danger of that."

"Really?" Theo challenged. "I've usually found love to be a bit messier than that."

She packed up her equipment. "Not in this case. This is not an instance where I have any plans to get back up on the horse that threw me, Pastor."

"Look at you, cowboy." Luke's cousin Witt came out from behind the cash register at the Blue Thorn Ranch Store, the retail portion of the ranch's business where they sold bison meat and other products. "I knew you were back in town, and I figured that massive appetite of yours would bring you in sooner or later."

"It's not like we don't have meat at home," Luke joked. "But you sure have gussied up the place. I've heard all about the new website, not to mention the food truck you have selling bison burgers in Austin. And then there's the—" he cast a derisive glance over at the section of the store that housed his sister Ellie's bison yarn goods "—mittens."

"Hey," said Witt, "don't knock the mittens. They were our best selling online product last year."

Luke picked one up, a little stumped as to why anyone would buy mittens knitted out of bison hair. He'd heard Ellie's speech about the marvelous qualities of bison yarn—heard it several times over, as a matter of fact—but he still didn't quite get point.

Then again, could he really judge? Had he done anything to bolster the family business? Gran's letting him have the guest-house amounted to taking family charity in his view, so he was doing worse than nothing. All the more reason to get back out there and ride his way into the top championships where the real money was.

"You run the food truck on top of managing the store and website, right?" Witt had expanded the Blue Thorn enterprise to include a bison burger food truck last year. Luke had met the truck's female chef—now Witt's fiancée—at Ellie's wedding. That was the same trip where he got into a fight with Tess. Not a slew of happy memories there.

Witt smiled. "Jana runs the truck. I run the marketing. We just added a second truck, so now I can joke I manage the fleet."

"Good for you." Again, more accomplishments from another branch of the family. Maybe coming home had been a bad idea.

"You'll be here for the wedding, won't you? October?"

It bugged him that some folks assumed he was staying. That he'd washed up his rodeo career for good when that wasn't the case at all. "I'll be out on the tour by then. Or at least following the tour, in training. But sure, I'll try to make it back."

Witt shouldn't have looked so surprised. "Back? You're going back to it? That soon?"

"Why shouldn't I?" Luke shot back. "I'm fine. I'm healing faster than anyone expected. Of course I'll be back…and soon."

Witt held up his hands. "Hey, hey, no harm no foul. I'm happy for you, man. I'd thought you were…"

"You thought *what*, exactly?" Luke challenged, feeling heat rise up his spine. The inkling that anyone thought he was finished in the rodeo just made him nuts. "Do you see any cane, any crutches? I'm fine. Fine and getting stronger."

"Okay," Witt said. "I didn't mean to imply anything. Jana and I just want you at the wedding, that's all."

"I'll try." Luke left without picking up the burgers his sister-in-law, Brooke, had asked for. They had enough bison meat at home and he didn't want to be in there anymore.

Chapter Seven

The shiny vehicle's door opened and a set of long legs extended out onto the gravel. Ruby took in the full picture almost as quickly as Luke ran his eyes up and down the statuesque brunette. Fancy white jeans tucked into fancy black boots, expertly mussed hair, curves that would stop a stampede. "Well, hello there, Luke Buckton!"

Pro Bull Rider Magazine had said they were sending a journalist, not a spokesmodel. Ruby felt three inches tall and nearly invisible. In ten minutes it would be as if she wasn't even there.

"You have to be Rachel Hartman," Luke rose from his chair on the ranch house lawn as if carried by the breeze, all effortless athletic grace. Of course, that was all for show, since they were taking a break from a series of challenging exercises that had had him breaking out in a sweat only ten minutes before. "I thought you were coming tomorrow."

"I was, but my other assignment ended early and a seat opened up on an Austin flight. Who needs a day at home to do laundry when I can get started on what could be the story of the year?"

"I don't know if the Gap House is ready for you," Ruby said as she stood up. "Did you check?" She'd kept her mouth shut about how glad she was the reporter was staying at the little inn in town rather than out here on the ranch. Twenty-four-hour media access had to be a bad thing, even for the likes of Luke.

"First thing I thought of—I'm all set. So there was no reason for me to wait another day. Hope that's all right. I probably should have called first, but I was on a roll."

I can just imagine, Ruby thought darkly. She told herself not to judge, but the gorgeous brunette smiling at Luke pressed every one of Ruby's buttons and there was no help for it.

"You must be the therapist. Ruby Sheldon, right?" Rachel turned and extended her hand. "I definitely want to spend a lot of time with you. I think your take on this would be fascinating to include."

"I'm not so sure," Ruby replied. "This

is Luke's story." *One I advised against but agreed to anyway. One I'm not sure will end well.*

"I disagree," Rachel tossed a head of perfect wavy hair but managed to offer what looked like a genuine smile. "It's the story of a comeback and the people who make it happen. That includes you. And the doctors who performed the surgeries that allowed Luke to heal. And probably whatever bull ends up underneath that cowboy. The whole thing's one great American heart-tugger of a drama. Besides," she leaned in to Ruby, "I want to know the secret for putting up with a guy like him. He doesn't strike me as anyone's favorite patient."

"Hey," Luke interjected, "I'm everyone's favorite patient."

Rachel cocked her head in Luke's direction. "Ah, that legendary bull rider humility. A virtue among virtues, huh?"

Ruby could almost laugh at that. Maybe this Rachel reporter wasn't the smitten buckle bunny Ruby had assumed she was. "Luke works hard. He knows what he wants and he's willing to do whatever it takes to get there. If anything, the hardest part is holding him back from overdoing it."

"I'll make two or three trips back here over

the next few weeks, and try not to get in the way." Rachel pulled out a notepad and pen. "Were you at a good stopping point?"

"We were just going to do some walking," Luke said, extending an arm. "It helps if I have something to hold on to."

Rachel rolled her eyes. "And there's that other legendary bull rider virtue."

"Overwhelming charm?" Luke's voice was silky smooth as he tucked Rachel's arm into the crook of his elbow.

"Overwhelming *something*," Rachel said. "Now how am I supposed to write anything down with you hanging on me like that?"

"You'll manage. I'll stop for a moment when I say something especially recordable." Luke looked over at Ruby. "Twenty minutes, right?"

"Fifteen," she corrected. "Steady pace, no running."

"I'll show you around the ranch," Luke said. "Ever seen a bison ranch up close before?"

Rachel threw Ruby one last glance before heading off with Luke. "I promise to have him back by curfew," she called, laughing.

Ruby watched them turn the corner of the barn, feeling like a large and dangerous train had just left the station without her. An unwelcome curl of jealousy wormed its way under her ribs. Part of her knew why Luke was doing this; charming the press had always been a gift of his. Another part of her felt the old sting of inadequacy rise up from a packed-away place.

"It's started, has it?"

Ruby turned to see Granny B scowling after Luke and his new escort as they made their way toward where the bison were fenced. She hadn't heard the old woman come up. "Seems so."

"She's awful pretty, that one." Granny pursed her lips. "That'll make it harder."

Ruby turned to her. "How do you mean?"

"I know my grandson. He'll be bent on impressing her. He'll do things he shouldn't, take extra chances to be dazzling. Never could keep that boy's feet on the ground."

Ruby had been searching for the right moment to ask. "Do you think he can do it, Granny B?"

The woman offered a resigned smile. "Does it matter what I think?"

"It does to me."

Granny B put a hand on Ruby's arm. "I think I'm glad you're here. If he does do it, you'll be a big part of the reason why. If he doesn't, it'll take all of us and then some to pick up the pieces." She gave Ruby's arm a squeeze. "I know one thing for sure—none of us could stop him. Never could once he set his mind to something." They were both quiet for a long moment before Granny B added, "I'm sorry, you know. For how things ended up between you back then."

How long had she waited to hear those words from this woman? "Thanks."

"Even if he's never said it, even if he's said the opposite, he knows what he did was wrong. I think he regrets it, too, even if he can't bring himself to admit it." Granny B released Ruby's arm and patted her on the shoulder. "You've got a special kind of strong to be here, I know it. I see it. He'll see it, too, when he comes to his senses."

Ruby turned to face Granny B. "I'm not looking to start up with Luke again, Granny B. I won't say it's entirely professional, but it's friendship, nothing else." A good therapist knew when something was too fragile to strain—and her heart just couldn't take being broken again.

"I'll see you in town for lunch tomorrow. Lolly's does good Southern cooking like you won't believe." Luke waved as Rachel Hartman folded those long legs into her car and drove off. He stared long after the car until his brother, Gunner, walked up behind him.

"I don't remember reporters looking like that," Gunner said.

"Yes, well, what goes for press around here leaves a lot to be desired. That right there is national magazine talent, not the livestock reporters I expect you're used to. Smart, too."

Gunner adjusted his hat. "Smart enough to see through your dazzle?"

"Very funny." He couldn't quite put a finger on the strange feeling in his gut. Or, more precisely, lack of feeling. Usually the numbness was only in his leg.

"What?" Gunner asked. "You look odd. Well, odder than usual."

"I'm just stumped, that's all."

"About what? Some long-legged beauty just signed on to follow your every move. I'd think you'd be thrilled."

Luke scratched his chin. "Yeah, me, too."

"You're not? She seems your type to me." Gunner looked at him as they started walking back toward the big house. "You worried she's gonna try to pull something on you?"

Every reporter always had an angle. His talent was usually the ability to play that angle to his advantage. Luke loved the press, and the press loved him. Usually. They hadn't paid much attention to him lately, and that bugged him, but the "off" feeling he had now wasn't about that. "Nah, she's seems on the up-and-up, actually. I think she'll do a good job."

"So what's the deal?"

Luke stopped walking and looked at his brother. "I don't like her."

"You just made a lunch date with her, and you don't like her?"

Luke ran one hand down his face. "She seems nice enough, but I don't *like* like her. I mean, earlier I would have, you know…"

Gunner gave a low laugh. "Been hitting on her within ten minutes of meeting her?"

It sounded so sleazy when Gunner put it that way. "Well, flirting, at least. Going all charming on her. Trying to get a date as well as an interview."

Stuffing his hands in his pockets, Gunner asked, "And that's not what you just did in planning to meet her at Lolly's? I don't see what you're getting at."

"I could have—gone all charming, that is—but I didn't really want to." Luke stared after the cloud of dust just settling on the ranch drive, genuinely stumped. "It didn't seem worth the effort. A while back I would have been pouring it on thick with a looker like her, and a reporter besides. Today I just couldn't seem to muster it up."

"She looked all 'mustered up' to me. You charmed her, believe me. You could probably charm a woman in your sleep, you know. It's like breathing to you. I don't know that you could stop yourself if you wanted to."

Luke gave his brother a glare. It wasn't his fault he was always a hit with the ladies and Gunner was always just the rebel. But then, it had worked out for Gunner in the long run, hadn't it? The perpetual loner now had a beautiful wife, a stepdaughter who thought he hung the moon, and an adorable baby son. Whereas Luke had…a lunch date with a woman who'd totally failed to capture his interest.

"Wait a minute…wait a minute," Gunner said, "I think I know what's going on here." He peered at Luke intently. "That knock on your head, it made you grow up. You've—" and he strung the next word out in a classic big brother tease "—matured. I wasn't sure it would ever happen. Watch out for a relapse, little brother, you never know when those can hit you."

"*I* could hit *you*," Luke shot back, knocking Gunner's hat off his head.

Gunner jogged over to where his hat tumbled across the lawn. "If you could catch me, that is," he called.

"Again, not worth the effort," Luke called as he veered left toward the guesthouse. He couldn't catch Gunner. Not yet. And he didn't really want to "catch" Rachel Hartman. What was up with that?

As he opened the guesthouse door, it struck him. Could it really be true? The great Luke Buckton had tired of buckle bunnies? Had grown jaded over the false, fawning beauties that used to be his favorite form of diversion?

Grown up?

Well, he was twenty-four. Stranger things had happened.

Chapter Eight

Wednesday morning, Luke stared at the vicious little contraption Ruby had shown him during their last session just before Rachel Hartman had arrived. Rachel had some conference call this morning, and he was glad to face the device without an audience. "I've named it," he growled to Ruby as she set it down on the floor. It looked like a giant blue blister, a half bubble of rubber that sat flat on the floor just waiting to tumble him over.

Ruby straightened up. "It has a name. It's a Bosu Balance Trainer."

"Well, I've renamed it. That thing's name is JetPack." He waited for her to make the connection.

It took her half a minute, but that look came into her eyes. The one that usually had "grow up" attached to it or some other maturity-soaked phrase. She'd been good at them at eighteen, she was a master at them now. "You've named a useful therapeutic device after the bull that threw you."

"Well, I hate that little blue thing." He did. Lots of his therapy made him feel stronger, like he was healing, but that nasty hunk of rubber took him down a peg every time he stepped on it.

"This isn't supposed to be fun and games. Therapy is hard work. The Luke Buckton I knew wasn't afraid of that."

"And I'm not now," he shot back. She would throw that phrase "the Luke Buckton I knew" in every once in a while because it got under his skin. Even though he knew she was manipulating him, he still rose to the bait every time. It bugged him how well she could play him, even though that's exactly why he'd asked her to come on board.

She stood on the other side of the thing. "Okay, cowboy, up on the little blue ball that threw you."

He kicked off his sneakers. He could do that now. Things were coming back to him, slower than he'd like, but coming back just the same. "Can I pop it once I master it? Gunner's got an axe in the barn with this thing's name on it."

Ruby didn't even flinch. "No. One hand today." Before, he'd needed to hold both her hands or the back of a chair to stay balanced on the thing. Evidently he'd graduated to one hand, which suited his plan perfectly. He walked over to the little dinette and picked up the large manila envelope Nolan had forwarded yesterday. "I've planned some distraction."

"I prefer you pay attention."

"I will. I'll be listening to you. You're going to read me my fan mail while I do my time on the blue beast." He set the envelope down on a nearby table, but not before reaching into it like a raffle bowl, fishing dramatically around until he pulled up a single envelope. "You read, I'll balance." He held out the rose-colored envelope, mildly amused to see the address written in a swirly feminine hand. Three-quarters of his fan mail came from women.

Ruby looked at the envelope, clearly came to the same conclusion about the author and broke the seal with an incredulous look. "If it will keep you from complaining the whole time…"

"Guaranteed complaint-free compliance. Fan mail is always entertaining reading."

She unfolded the pink paper. "For you

maybe." She extended a hand, which Luke took and stepped onto the jiggly rubber ball. It was like trying to stand on one of Gran's Jell-O salads. It only put him half a foot off the ground, but he'd tilted clean off the dastardly little thing more times than he could count.

"Dear Luke," Ruby began.

Women always started "Dear Luke" while men and kids, when they wrote, usually addressed him "Dear Mr. Buckton" or "Mr. Luke."

"I've been praying for you every day since your accident." Ruby's scowl softened a bit. "That's actually rather sweet."

"We ought to write her back and tell her it's working," Luke replied, shifting his weight from side to side the way Ruby instructed. "Go on."

Ruby returned to reading. *"I think you'd be on your way to champion if JetPack hadn't done what he did. You're very brave to do what you do, and I love watching you. Ray Knight is a good rider, but he wouldn't be in first place right now if you were still on the tour."*

"She's smart, this…one," Luke commented, his remark cut off by a momentary loss of balance.

Ruby held his hand steady, waiting patiently for him to regain his footing. When he nodded, she looked back at the letter. *"'Of course, you're far better looking than Ray, so there's that.'"*

"Well, there *is* that. Ray's got a face only a mama could love, even if he can ride."

"'I want you to know,'" Ruby continued, *"'that I do hope very much you recover soon so we can all see you in the arena again. You're amazing, and you're my favorite.'* That line's punctuated with five hearts, in case you were wondering."

"Five hearts is very motivating."

"Who knew?" She peered at the bottom of the letter. *"'All my love to my brave hero, Christi.'* With an *i*. And each *i* has a little heart for the dot."

"Seven hearts. I'm full of inspiration."

"You're full of something, that's for sure. But you did just do a whole minute without griping. You might be on to something."

Of course he was on to something. Fan mail was fun, stomping around on this silly wobbly ball was not. Luke nodded toward the envelope. "Read me another."

She went through half a dozen letters, the writers ranging from cutesy teenagers to army veterans, from smitten young women and admiring up-and-coming riders. This was fuel for him. Sure, he loved attention, but being looked up to always seemed to bring out a drive in him, a hunger to show the world what he could do. Plus, it gave Ruby a sense of all the people watching and waiting for him to get back in the arena. This was bigger than just him, and he needed to make her understand that.

He was patting himself on the back for the cleverness of his idea—and how quickly it had made the time on the balance ball fly—when she pulled a final letter from the envelope. "Two minutes more," Ruby said, genuinely smiling. "Time for one last dose of admiration."

A child's lettering filled the front of the envelope. Ruby unfolded two sheets of lined notebook paper filled with the same writing.

She held out her hand for Luke to take it and continue his movements. *"'Dear Mr. Buckton, I want to know...'"* She stopped, her eyebrows furrowing as her face went a bit pale.

"Go on," he said, shifting his weight as required.

"No," she said quickly, "I think we're done."

"No we're not. I'm not skimping on this. Keep going."

Ruby placed the letter facedown onto the table.

"Hold on there. What's up?" When she didn't answer, he stood still on the ball and squeezed her hand. "Read it, Ruby."

She pulled her hand free and began stuffing it back into the larger envelope. "You don't need to read that one."

Luke stepped down off the ball. Apparently the letter said something negative. He felt a pang at that, but pushed it back. Being a celebrity meant taking the bad with the good— he couldn't just ignore the parts he didn't like. "I read them all. Let's hear it." If he was the type of man to run from something that might hurt him, he'd never be able to make his living climbing on the backs of angry bulls.

Slowly, she retrieved the letter. She looked up at him once more, clearing her throat twice before she read: *"Dear Mr. Buckton, I want to know how you call yourself a real cowboy after giving up like you have.'"* Ruby hesitated, choking on the accusation that sunk to Luke's gut like a load of stone. *"I broke my leg last fall when my horse threw me, but my dad told me to get back up and ride just as soon as my cast was off. So why aren't you back? I never heard nothing about you breaking anything, so where are you? Lots of people look up to you, and I used to...'* Ruby's voice cracked just a tiny heartbreaking bit right there, and Luke felt his body go still and cold. *"...but now I think you're just scared. My dad says that's no way to be a champion. Why are you letting Ray Knight take what oughta be yours? You probably don't even read your fan mail, so I won't be surprised if you don't answer me.'* She looked up at him with glistening, pain-filled eyes. *"Your former fan, Eddie Parker."'*

It wasn't the first mean letter he'd ever gotten, but this one cut so deep he couldn't seem to drag air into his lungs. He wanted to laugh it off, to give her some quick and witty comeback, but his throat was closed up too tight for words.

Instead he snatched it from her hands, wadding the words up in his fist as he turned... and tripped on his bad leg, sending him careening into the table and sending the letters flying all over the room.

He didn't hold back when he slammed his fist into the table as he got up, even though he could feel the bruise forming on the heel of his hand within seconds of the blow. He just wished he'd held back the look he gave Ruby, for her face dissolved into a look of pity so deep it made him want to growl.

"Luke..." Ruby stammered, "I don't know what to say."

"What's there to say?" he practically shouted back, scrambling to upright himself with such ferocity that she knew not to try and help. Pain and anger radiated off him in dark, sharp waves.

"He's got it all wrong," she offered, feeling like the words weren't anywhere near enough. "Who'd write something like that?" She knew Luke got fan mail—bull riders were big stars even on the smaller circuits—but hate mail? From young boys? She didn't think the world was that cruel. "Who'd let their son write something like that to an injured man?"

Ruby knew instantly she'd chosen the wrong words. Luke visibly flinched at the word *injured*, the fire in his eyes doubling in strength. "Some days it rots to be a role model, sweetheart. People get ugly when you disappoint them."

Ugly. That was the word for the letter she'd just read. Some of the star-struck letters were cute or silly or syrupy, but this last one was ugly. Ruby turned the envelope over to see the return address, some part of her itching to go ring that brat's doorbell and give him a piece of her mind about the virtues of compassion and kindness. *It's a good thing he lives hours away, Lord*, she prayed, *or I'd do something I'd regret*.

"We're done," Luke's words were dark and short.

"You can't let one mean boy's letter…"

"I said *we're done*!" Luke shouted, not meeting her eyes as he eased himself into a chair.

It felt dangerous to leave him like this. *He's angry enough to do anything*, she thought. "We can be done," she said softly, "but I don't think I should go."

"You should." He looked anywhere but at her. Did that boy have any idea of the senseless pain he'd inflicted?

"Maybe, but I won't. He doesn't get to do that to you, Luke. He's wrong."

Luke just shrugged. Ruby remembered how Luke's father, Gunner Buckton Sr. never missed an opportunity to show any of this children his disappointment. Gunner Sr. was an angry man who took his failings out on his children, driving them all off as the ranch slowly slipped into failure. Only Gran's plea to Luke's older brother, Gunner Jr., had brought the eldest back onto the ranch after his father's death and enabled the turnaround Blue Thorn Ranch enjoyed now.

She grasped for something to say, some way to undo the damage. All the progress Luke had made seemed to melt off his frame, as if his body were sinking back toward woundedness right in front of her eyes.

"It's the bravest thing in the world to choose to heal, Luke. Any coward can let an injury define him." She closed the gap between them and tried to hold his gaze. "To walk straight on, into the limitations of an injury, accept them and then face them down? Like you've done? Like you're doing? There's no braver thing."

He lifted his gaze with something that looked too much like resignation. Ruby found it far more unsettling than the anger that had consumed him a moment ago. "Oh, yeah," he said, sarcasm dripping from his tone. "Look at me, big brave Luke Buckton on his silly blue ball."

Ruby grabbed his arm. "So that's it? You ignore me, you disregard your doctors, you pay no attention to the people who want what's best for you when we tell you that you're pushing yourself too hard, but you give some mean little kid the power to knock you off your treatment? The Luke I knew would be stomping mad, just itching to put that brat in his place. We need that man, because that man is the only one strong enough to do what you're aiming to do."

Luke shot up out of the chair faster than she'd ever seen him move. "You think I'm not mad?" He was close to yelling.

Ruby felt her spine straighten, felt her resolve meet his, glare for glare. "I think you're not mad *enough*!" Somehow, in the space of two sheets of paper, she'd moved from trying to hold him back to seeing how he needed to go at this full force. All-out, all or nothing. If he did that and failed, he stood a chance of healing. But if he didn't, if he went down without a fight—he'd never be the same. He'd never be whole. He'd be just the man who used to be Luke Buckton.

She knew that because she understood him, saw how his heart and soul worked, just the same as she had back when she loved him.

Because a part of her still cared.

Ruby grabbed her file and thrust her hand through the loop that carried the balance ball, whacking Luke's chair as she yanked it off the floor. It was heavy, but right now she was so emotional she felt as if she could fling it clear across the bison pastures.

"Find that man, Luke. Make sure he's here when I come back on Friday." She banged the guesthouse door so loud she saw Gran coming to the front door of the ranch house to see what was the matter.

"Don't bother!" he roared, from the doorway.

She turned back after tossing her gear into the trunk of her car. "Try and stop me!"

Chapter Nine

Ruby turned over for the twentieth time that night, staring at the too-bright moonlight that came through her apartment window. It had been a waste of time to try to sleep. Good thing Luke had been her last appointment of the day—she'd have been useless with another patient, as preoccupied as she was.

Every time she closed her eyes she saw the ugly words in those childish block letters. *Why*? She kept asking God. *What's the purpose of such cruelty? And from someone so young?*

Though he'd clearly been hurt, Luke hadn't seemed all that surprised at the letter. Did he get many like that? She couldn't pretend to know what it was like to have that kind of notoriety—and today showed her she was glad for it. It made her think. Had Luke been right in presuming she couldn't handle what the rodeo life could dish out? If people were that mean to Luke—who had so many attractive and admirable qualities not to mention good looks—what would they do to the likes of her?

It struck an old, raw nerve. *I thought I'd gained more self confidence than this.* She hated how second-guessing Luke's years-old departure took her back to the young, tender—and yes, overly sensitive—version of herself. It felt as if the new, older Ruby was just a shell built over the younger Ruby. A shell that could crack and fall away at any moment.

That's not true, she told herself. *You know it's not true. God's shown you over and over it's not true. You can't always trust the way you feel, you know that. Lord, show me a way to battle this.*

Her cell phone rang despite the late hour. It made her jump—she always kept it on in case Mama had an emergency with Grandpa. She scrambled for the phone—no one ever called at 1:30 a.m. with good news—startled to see Luke's name on the screen.

"Are you up?" His voice sounded different. Lower, huskier.

"I am now. Well, actually, I was lying

awake so yeah." She pushed the hair out of her face and sat up. "Are you okay?"

There was a pause on the phone, and the sound of him shifting. "Can we talk?"

Ruby started to reach for the light, but instead walked over to the window. The moon was bright enough tonight; she didn't need to turn on a lamp. She pulled aside the drapes and then backed instantly away, yelping when she saw Luke's truck on the street in front of the duplex where she lived. He was sitting on the back of the open tailgate, looking up at her window.

"How long have you been out there?" she gasped, clutching at the ratty T-shirt she'd been sleeping in.

"About an hour. At first I wasn't gonna call, then it was like I had to."

She fumbled around her bedroom for a pair of jeans and a shirt. "I'll come down." There were more reasons than just the stairs why she didn't want him coming up. This space belonged to her life beyond him, and she wasn't ready to let him inside.

Ruby hung up, got dressed, washed her face, pulled a brush through her hair and threw on a pair of shoes. "Oscar, honey," she told her dog, "you make a lousy watchdog. I'll be back." On a last impulse she pulled two cans of sparkling lemonade from the fridge and walked down the stairs.

Luke looked rattled. The bristling anger of this afternoon had mostly deflated, leaving him with a lost quality that tugged dangerously at her. Stumped for what to say, she simply hiked up to sit a safe distance from him on the tailgate. She set one of the drinks next to him, popping the tab on the other.

"You still drink this stuff?" Sparkling lemonade had been a favorite of hers since childhood. Luke used to kid her about it, how she drank this particular brand on nearly a daily basis all through high school.

Ruby nodded, taking a long drink before saying "You couldn't sleep either?"

He settled back against one side of the pickup, stretching his bad leg out across the expanse of the tailgate so that one showy cowboy boot pointed up inches from her knee. The boots really were just like him— stunning, but in an outlandish sort of way.

"I used to be better about that sort of thing. You know, laugh it off, make wisecracks about dumb kids, jealous cowboys and mean old coots."

That confirmed her suspicion that such letters had happened before. "What makes someone write something like that?"

"Oh, every rider's got a different theory about why folks do that kind of thing." Luke opened his own drink. "Nolan always says if you ain't making someone mad you're probably not doing anything at all. 'Better to get a rise than to get ignored' he always says. 'Course, no one's writing to call him a disappointment and a coward."

"You're not a coward."

He took a long swig. "But I am a disappointment. Even to me. This stuff is awful, you know. Like drinking candy."

"How does coping with a huge adversity like this make you a disappointment? And don't give me the old 'cowboy up' bit—it doesn't apply and you know it."

"Doesn't matter if I know it. All they see is the guy who didn't get back up." He leaned back and looked up at the moon, round and brilliant in one corner of the sky. "I've dropped out of sight, Ruby, and that's the kiss of death in my business."

"And all this business with that woman and the magazine is going to change that?"

"That's the plan."

None of this was news. "Why are you here, Luke?"

He shifted his weight and returned his gaze to her. Those blue eyes stood out like beacons in the sharp shadows of the moonlit night. "Best Eyes" the yearbook superlatives section had called him. Magnetic. "Believe it or not, I came to apologize."

Now this was news. Luke Buckton rarely did regrets or apologies. She offered no reply.

"I was a jerk to you today. It took some time, but life has taught me to recognize such things. I have added a few skills sincc…well since back then."

Neither one of them had come up with the right words to refer to their high school relationship. It had been love—as deep and true as it came at that age—but that didn't help to find the words that worked now.

"That letter hurt you. Hurting people do damage, usually to whatever's in reach." Ruby didn't want to venture in the territory of the deep hurt he'd caused her back then. "I still don't understand why anyone would think it's okay to say such things. Whatever happened to not kicking a man when he's down?"

His body flinched at her use of the phrase. "Is that what I am? Down? Off limits for anything but pity?"

He really did have a hair trigger for anything related to his injury.

"Down is not the same as out. You are injured and healing. You are overcoming a set-back that I expect would finish men with half your determination." And, because she'd decided not to pity the man, she added, "And you said you were here to apologize."

"I am."

She crossed her arms. "Where I come from," she began, fully aware they came from the same town currently asleep all around them, "an apology contains the words *I'm sorry.*" If he said he'd learn to recognize when he was being a jerk, then it was time to prove he'd also learned what real men do with such a realization.

Luke Buckton let precious few people order him around. Back in high school, she'd gotten away with calling him on faults that might have earned other people a shouting match. It had been years, but he'd shown she still had that right. They both knew it was a big reason why she was treating him.

Luke sat up straight, adjusting his hat as if making a formal proclamation. "Ruby Sheldon, I'm sorry for being a jerk to you today. I took my anger out on you when you were trying to help me. That was wrong. Please forgive me."

Some part of her wanted to offer a wise-crack about words she'd never expected to hear out of his mouth, but Ruby settled for a small smile and a "toast" with her can of lemonade. "Apology accepted."

He extended a hand. Not sideways for a shake, but palm up to take hers. Ruby hesitated a moment before slipping her hand into his; it felt like toeing up to a line that ought not to be crossed. His fingers wrapped warm and solid around hers, his thumb finding its way to the back to make lazy circles in a way that sent tingles to the back of her neck. Just like high school, only different. Back then, Luke held her hand to "woo" her closer, to spark something more. Right now, in the moonlight after such a painful day, it was just a gesture of friendship.

At least that's what she told herself.

Luke texted Ruby for the third time Friday morning. He'd worn a hole in the guesthouse floor waiting for her to reply, his patience all but exhausted. He had to tell someone, and he really wanted that someone to be Ruby, even if she wasn't due for another three hours. Why wouldn't she answer her phone? He'd typed *URGENT* and *IMPORTANT* in the last two messages and was ready to type *CALL ME RIGHT THIS MINUTE!!!!* with an eighth-grader's dousing of exclamation points if he thought it would do any good.

He did another lap through the house, confirmed his findings, gave himself a wincing grin in the bathroom mirror, and glared at the phone sitting all too quietly on his kitchen table. *Come on Ruby...*

At last the device buzzed, skittering on the table for only half a second before he scooped it up and hit the button to accept the call. "It hurts!" he yelped into the phone before Ruby said a single word.

"What?"

"It hurts. I woke up this morning and my leg hurt. Not all the time, and only when I do certain things, but Ruby, *it hurts*."

He felt the sound of her gasp all the way through his chest. "Where? How?"

"Little sparks of pain, shooting up from the heel. And others shooting down from the small of my back. It hurts, Ruby. It hurts!" He turned the corner by his couch so fast he tripped, his heart doing leaps at the jabs of pain that shot up his leg when he landed sideways on the couch.

"Are you okay?"

"I just fell down. And it hurt." He leaned his head back on the couch arm and fought the urge to whoop. "Bring it on. I want to be reaching for the aspirin by supper. I want to ache so bad tears run down my face."

"If sensation is coming back then that's wonderful news, Luke. But you don't want to push it. Be careful until I get there, will you? I just finished up at Doc Nelson's office, I can be there in fifteen minutes."

"You'll come now?" He really wanted her to. He wanted to celebrate with the whole world right now, but most especially with Ruby.

"As fast as I can. Try to stay seated, will you?"

He scrambled back up off the couch, ignoring how his knee buckled when he did. He hurt—what did anything else matter right now? "Not a chance. I promise not to dance or run the mile, but *no way* am I sitting down for this."

"*Try* to take it easy? Just for the next fifteen minutes?"

Luke stuck his foot out, and then stomped it on the ground, luxuriating in the pricks of pins and needles that shot up his leg. This was pain, and he knew how to conquer pain. Ruby had done it. He'd known she would. He'd known he could count on her. "Get here. Speed and I'll pay for the ticket. Or I'll ask Ellie's husband, Nash, to get you off—having the sheriff for a brother-in-law ought to be good for something."

She laughed, and he remembered how much he liked her laugh. "I'll get there when I get there—and legally, thank you. Just don't be on a horse or a bike when I drive up."

It was a good thing the vintage motorcycle in Gran's barn wasn't rideable. The idea of racing down the road, feeling his leg burn when he leaned into the left-hand turns, lured like candy. Maybe he'd have Gunner wheel it out and he'd just sit on it to watch her eyes pop out of her head as she drove up. A million possibilities kept going off in his brain like strobe lights—flickers in rapid succession. Like the delicious pain in his left leg.

Nolan. Should he call Nolan? Rachel from *Pro Bull Rider Magazine* was coming back into town on Monday for a second interview—think of what he could show off by then if things kept up the way they were!

I'm back. His whole body was shouting it as if all the determination blocked by the numbness was letting loose like a floodgate. *I'm back.*

He walked—okay, he was limping but that's because it *hurt*—past the trashcan and caught sight of the crumpled letter from nasty little "former fan" Eddie Parker. Yesterday, he'd decided the kid didn't deserve an answer. He had nothing to say to that brat, except maybe a few sharp words to the mom or dad who hadn't had the decency to stop him from mailing it. Luke thought of his sweet niece, Audie—the kindest, most encouraging kid he'd ever known—and looked up on his fridge to see drawings from the girl. Imagine—give a kid some paper and writing tools and look how differently they could use them. Audie encouraged him, Eddie shot him down.

Luke fished the letter from the basket and spread it on the table. "You're going to hear from me, Eddie. I don't know what yet, or how, and I get that you're just a kid, but you're a mean kid who just picked on the wrong guy."

Gran. Nolan could wait, even Rachel could wait, but Gran needed to hear the news. Luke made for the guesthouse door to cross the yard over to the big house, but stopped at the sight of the Bible Gran had left for him on the table by the door.

She'd left it two weeks ago, and he'd not touched it. He and God weren't exactly chummy before the accident, and he hadn't been in any mood to warm up the relationship since. Still, it wasn't hard to predict what Gran's response to this leap forward in his healing would be: she'd call it an answer to prayer.

Was it?

It was easy to dismiss the Almighty's hand in his recovery when he *wasn't* recovering. While he hadn't turned his anger toward blaming the Lord—God owed him no favors, he'd not merited any blessings, that's for sure—he sure hadn't seen any signs of mercy or grace in his injury. Yet Gran, Ruby, and even persistent Pastor Theo went on about how trials like this bring folks closer to their Maker.

He'd come as close to his Maker—meeting Him, that is—as he wanted to get when Jet-Pack decided to lob him into that metal railing. After all, it was one of "God's creatures" who'd catapulted him to his demise, not the recklessness everyone always warned would be his undoing.

What had healed him? Who had healed him? Ruby? Prayers? Gran? Time? God? His own stubborn resolve? Luke craved a concrete answer, but came up empty. He might never know the answer to that question, which left the uneasy possibility that either prayers or God had played a part. It felt like walking across the lawn would just open the door for Gran to go all "grace of God" on him, and he preferred to pin this victory on his own shoulders.

She loves you. They all do—or at least that's what they keep saying. Go give them the good news and let them think whatever they want. Who cares how or why those nerves are working again? It happened, and that's all that matters.

With a resolute yank, Luke pulled the guesthouse door open. Delighted to leave the cane on its hook by the door, he put on his hat and set to strolling in painful splendor across the Blue Thorn Ranch lawn.

He made it halfway before his leg buckled and he went down like a rock.

A furious, cheated, numb-legged rock.

Chapter Ten

Luke was so excited.

He was *too* excited. She was thrilled he'd recovered some sensation—it really was good news—but she could hear the absolute victory in his voice, as if all the work was over. That kind of thinking with this kind of injury was dangerous.

He deserved a victory. He deserved progress. And she'd been praying that something positive would show up to undo all the damage of Eddie Parker's letter. She was glad for this, glad for him.

But she also knew Luke. Give the man an inch and he took not just one mile, but three, and refused to accept the possibility of setbacks. Recovery didn't work like that. She'd tried to make him understand that his progress would often be one step forward, two steps back, three steps forward, but he didn't really listen.

Make it stick, Lord. Give him this, will You? I know You're using this to get through to him, but he could just as easily push You away. Despite all her prayers, and all the people she knew were praying and waiting for good news from Luke, she couldn't shake the feeling of dread that iced down her spine as she hit the intercom for the Blue Thorn Ranch gate.

Granny B, answered, not Luke. "I thought Luke said you were coming this afternoon."

Why wasn't Luke over at the big house whooping it up with the family about his good news? The ice in her spine spread around to her ribs.

"Oh, mercy, did he fall and call you? He's sitting on the guesthouse steps. He doesn't look good. What happened?"

There wasn't an easy way to explain it. "I don't know yet. Is he upright?"

"He's sitting, holding his leg I think, with a look so dark I'm glad I'm all the way over here. Should I go see if he's okay?"

"No, I think I know what's going on. Leave him be, but pray. I think he just found out he's not in control of his own healing, and I doubt that's going down easy."

"I'll say." Granny B tsked. "God sure is doing some hard work in him right now. Breaks my heart to watch. Best you get on up here and see what you can do." With that, the intercom clicked off and the mechanical gate whirred open.

Ruby's stomach tightened as she wound her car up the long drive. She'd known this moment was coming. At some point Luke would have to face the truth that he couldn't simply grit his way back to bull riding. He'd have to face the terrifying prospect he might not get back at all. *I trust Your timing, Lord, but this feels all too soon. Help me know what to do.*

Luke looked like he might dissolve. The set of his shoulders pressed down with an all-too-foreign air of helplessness, his face not pulled tight in anger, but sagging in frustration. It was the attitude she'd seen the day of Eddie's letter, only ten times as strong. Her heart ached for him, for what he was enduring. Whether or not it was a necessary step in healing, Granny B was right: it was gut-wrenching to watch.

She got out of the car slowly, glad she'd dismissed her impulse to stop by Lolly's and get two slices of celebratory apple pie—Luke's favorite flavor. Today wasn't anything to celebrate—at least not anymore.

He did not look up at her. In fact, he seemed so folded in on himself she couldn't rightly say he even knew she had arrived. Out of the corner of her eye she saw Granny B move away from the kitchen window.

Poor Luke—he went all the way to the heights, but that gave him such a long way to fall. A man who does everything at 110 percent is as lethal as he is mesmerizing. The air around him bristled with the frustration of a man defying surrender to forces he could not control. His breath came in tight pushes, his fingers fisted and then spread, his jaw worked.

She sat down a small distance away on his good side. *Sometimes you can't speak peace, you can only bear witness to pain.* Those were Mama's words as together they watched Daddy die, surrendering to the damaged liver bent on taking Daddy's whole body down with it. They were doing it now with Grandpa, even though his demise was more slow and so much more peaceful. *I spend so much time bearing witness to pain, Lord. Right now it feels more like a curse than a gift.*

Finally, as his breathing eased up and the fingers stilled against his thigh, Ruby felt safe to speak. "It happens this way," she said softly. "It's still progress."

She wasn't surprised when he balked. "Not to me."

She was tempted to ask "Does it hurt now?" But she didn't really need to know the answer. He was in terrible pain—did it matter whether it was physical pain in his leg or the kind so much harder to heal? She simply said, "It is to me."

They sat in silence for a while longer. "I was so sure." Disappointment sagged his words into something closer to a moan. She held out her hand, as he had done on the tailgate, and he slid his hand into hers. There was no life, no energy in his fingers. She squeezed them anyway, feeling her lashes dampen with the heartbreak of his struggle. Luke at battle was a challenge, but Luke defeated hollowed out the part of her heart that would always belong to him.

"We just don't know how these things work," she offered, squeezing his hand again and still finding it lifeless. "Nerves don't always go online all at once—sometimes it's like a light bulb flickering on and off. Sometimes it goes in circles. That's why I say it takes such courage." She sighed. "If I could draw you a straight line to what you want, I would. But I can't, Luke. And neither can you."

"It felt so good to feel it, you know? It was like there was a rocket going off in my leg." Emotion thickened his voice. "After so long of…nothing."

"It is good news, even if it feels like torture right now."

The dramatic word turned his face toward her, and Ruby nearly gasped at the empty look in his eyes. "It's torture to have it dangled in front of me like that. I thought the pain meant it could work now. But…" He took his left hand and pounded the leg once or twice before she reached over him and stilled the punches.

It brought her close to him, and she gave in to the impulse to pull him into her arms. It was odd, that moment, for in all their time together he had always been the one to pull her in. She'd never been the kind of girl to flirt; he'd always pursued her. His strong arms would find her at school or around town or across the kitchen table, and she'd let herself be swept in. It was so gloriously, youthfully romantic.

This embrace was the opposite of that. It was, as Mama said, a "bearing witness," a bearing up. Older, harder, and then again, somehow softer. At this moment, it was she who was the stronger one, she who pursued as she tried to haul him out of the dark hole his reckless optimism had thrown him into. Ruby the therapist could recount the dozens of times she'd warned him how fickle nerves could be, how inconsistent his recovery would progress, but none of that mattered to the heart breaking next to hers. What he needed now was Ruby the friend.

Rachel Hartman eyed Luke above her notepad Monday afternoon. "Tell me, what is it about you cowboys that lets you do what you do?"

Luke rested his bad leg on the fence and scratched his chin. He'd been asked some version of this question by every version of a reporter from disbelieving eggheads to flirtatious correspondents. As such, he'd developed a standard reply—always accompanied by his most charming grin. "Well now, I do lots of fascinating things. Can you be a bit more specific?"

As media tactics go, it had it uses. The answer usually told Luke what it was the reporter was looking for. Some wanted personal heart-tugging stories. Others wanted to take the sport down a peg or two as just a heap of rowdy recklessness. Others—mostly the pretty ones—were just hinting to take the story off the page into something more interpersonal.

Rachel Hartman was smart, good-looking, but a city slicker of a gal who either dropped her Southern drawl or never had one. He was curious to find out just what she was looking for. "Get up on something bent on killing you," she clarified.

"You could say that about several sports. I had a buddy who moved up north to join the snowboarding circuit, and I'd say he gets up on something fixing to do him in every time he competes."

Rachel narrowed one eye. "A mountain is not actively trying to harm a skier."

Luke adjusted his hat. "Tell that to the surgeon who had to put Jake's leg back together with a handful of metal plates."

She wrote something down on her pad. "And what's holding your leg together?"

It was a tricky question, especially after Friday. He hadn't quite yet figured out a satisfactory answer. "The bones are fine. I got a nerve or two stomped on that's taking a bit of work to get up and running, that's all."

"So you've lost sensation in your left leg?" The way she said "lost" sounded far too final.

"It's not paralyzed, if that's what you're implying. As you can see, I walk just fine. Lots of times it doesn't hurt at all, other times it feels like someone set it on fire." That was putting a coat of shine on the infuriating combination of pain and numbness, but it was a good line for the press. "So while dancing might be a bit of a reach at the moment, I can always experiment for the sake of journalistic integrity." He'd gotten away with so many innuendoes and crazy suggestions by tacking the phrase "for journalistic integrity" onto the end that Nolan had begun to call it "The Luke Buckton 'bless your heart.'"

"Do you feel ready to ride?"

That was the million-dollar question, wasn't it? After all, it was why she was here. "I'll get there," he said, making a show of testing his leg.

"Have you ridden yet?"

A horse, yes. Gunner had let him ride around the ranch with him Sunday afternoon, and that felt like a gift of normalcy even if his brother watched closely to make sure he could stay in the saddle. But a bull? That wasn't something he was going to test until he was sure he'd succeed. Could he get to the point where even a questionable leg could hold him for the eight seconds he needed? He had to.

An exhibition ride now would set him up to hit the ground with a full plate of sponsors next year. *Just one more good season. That's all I really need.*

Luke evaded her query. "If you ask me, the question is have *you* ridden yet? Let's saddle you up and I'll show you some more of the family ranch." He made sure there was just enough challenge to his gaze before adding, "You can ride, can't you? They didn't just hire some pretty spectator from New York or anything did they?"

She looked as if she'd heard that one before. "Colorado. No drawl, but plenty of horses. And yes, I'd love to see the ranch. Plus, Paul here can get some great shots." She'd brought a photographer with her this time.

Luke led her to the horse barn where he had asked the ranch foreman, Billy Flatrock, to saddle up a pair of horses before Gunner could weigh in to the contrary. "Caramel's an easy mount." He doubled his drawl. "You won't even scuff up your boots none."

She tucked her notebook in the large leather bag she carried. "I can handle myself on a horse, Mr. Buckton."

"Luke," he corrected. Sure, he was pouring on the charm, but he was going to do anything he could to make sure this feature painted him in the best possible light. He needed Rachel Hartman on his side.

Billy tipped his hat as he led Caramel to the wooden box that would allow Rachel to mount up easily. Under other circumstances, Luke would have helped her up himself. Hoisting a lady up onto a horse had been a favorite trick of his for getting close to a woman. These days, he was neither in any shape to trust her weight on his legs, nor was he as fond of tricks. Even his appetite for the dreamy, gushing female fan letters had waned.

"While I love a wild ride as much as the next cowboy," he called back as he stepped into the stirrup with his good leg and threw the weaker one over Dash, "it's best we don't gallop around the bison. Gunner likes to keep 'em calm." The gallop bit was a half truth. Gunner did value peace and calm for his herd, but the "no gallop" rule was a convenience more for Luke's leg than for bison bliss. "Paul, Billy can take you out in the truck."

He'd hoped this little field trip would direct the conversation to his family heritage rather than his physical state, but Rachel steered the conversation back to where she wanted it. "To what do you owe your remarkable recovery?"

"Grace of God, good genes and excellent therapy." He and Nolan had crafted the first two elements of his answer, the third Luke had added as his way of thanking Ruby for her tolerance and persistence. He wasn't fool enough to ignore what a pain he was as a patient.

"Why didn't you head off to some sophisticated city rehab center?" Rachel asked.

"I love an audience, but not for this. Who doesn't like to head home when you've got a challenge ahead of you?" Another line Nolan had written. He gestured out over the pastures. "Beautiful, don't you think?"

"Gorgeous. No bulls?"

"Just the bison kind. Even *I'm* not fool enough to try riding one of those."

"Have you been back on a bull yet?"

"While I'm not fond of JetPak, I respect him. I want to do this right, and that means not riding him until everyone thinks I'm ready."

"You'll have to pick a date soon. What if your ride is scheduled and you're not ready?"

He flashed his best smile at Rachel. "Why discuss what won't ever happen?"

Chapter Eleven

"Is that how you keep up on patients now?" Lana stood over Ruby as she sat at the window table waiting for their weekly lunch at Lolly's. Ruby went to stuff the phone back in her handbag, embarrassed that she'd used the time waiting for Lana's return from the ladies' room to pull up Luke's social media page. She'd found three photos of him and an update that he was hosting *Pro Bull Rider Magazine's* Rachel Hartman for a ride around the ranch. The photos were beautiful. Stunning scenery and two photogenic personalities. The sight set off a wiggle of uncertainty in her stomach.

"No, don't put it away," Lana said. "Let me see."

"Well," said Lana as Ruby turned her phone to show her mentor. "So that's the reporter who's covering your treatment of Luke? She's a looker all right. No wonder she's in television."

"She writes for a magazine," Ruby corrected, taking the phone back and shoving it to the bottom of her handbag. "And she's nice." *And beautifully dressed, well spoken and sophisticated.* The photos had unleashed an unexpected curl of envy in Ruby's stomach. That was why he'd left her behind.

Lana sat down opposite Ruby at the table. "Awfully flashy for Martins Gap."

Ruby could already see where Lana was headed with this. "His life isn't here anymore. I'm not sure it ever was—he was always chomping at the bit to get out. The Blue Thorn isn't home, it's just a detour brought about by his injury. I mean, he's still staying in the ranch guesthouse even though he can climb stairs now—says it all, doesn't it?"

"So, once he's healed, he's gone." Lana leaned in. "You've told me your personal history with him. Have you been able to keep it professional?"

"Of course I have. You know, I've dreaded his return all these years, and now I'm over that. I won't say I wasn't anxious about treating him as a patient, but look at what I've been able to accomplish." Ruby unrolled her silverware from the napkin and settled the red checkered square neatly in her lap.

"So" Lana said as she did the same, "no worries about anything wandering into personal territory? None at all?"

"None."

"I find that hard to believe. Be honest with yourself. Let's get this out in the open so we can deal with it. Do you feel anything for the man?"

Ruby hesitated. She wanted to deny it, but it was harder to lie to Lana than to lie to herself. "Maybe."

"I'm not going to berate you for that, Ruby. You were serious with him once. You're working closely, and in close quarters. That history doesn't just disappear into thin air."

"He's still the driven, reckless, rocket of a man who launched himself out of Martins Gap in a blaze of 'I'm too big for this town,' convinced all the while that I deserved to be left behind." She fiddled with her silverware. "A walking danger zone, even if we are friends."

"*Just* friends…" Lana didn't look convinced.

Ruby let her hands fall into her lap. "I feel like…he's changed."

"It's been six years. Of course he's changed. The question is how much?"

"The smart part of me knows the answer is 'not enough.'"

Lana rested her chin in her hands. "Wouldn't it be great if we always listened to the smart parts of ourselves? I'll have your back if you decide you shouldn't be treating him. Based on what you've told me, that man knows just how to get to you."

Ruby resented Lana's questioning, but the truth was her partner was right to be concerned.

"I understand the dangers, Lana, really I do." Ruby leaned in. "But it goes both ways, which is the very thing that has helped me make such progress with Luke. I know it's why he fixed it so I would be his therapist."

"You mean he *manipulated* it so you'd be his therapist. An average person would have just asked, you know."

No one could call Luke Buckton "average."

"I would have said no."

"And I'm saying maybe you *should* have said no."

"But I didn't. I thought you always told me my best asset was that I'll never give up or walk away when it gets hard."

"That's true."

Ruby accepted her tuna melt when it arrived. "If I am able to get Luke to functionality, it would be a huge professional victory for us. Haven't we always said we want to convince doctors their patients can have choices outside of Austin for first-class care as well as in the city? What makes that case better than Luke Buckton's highly visible recovery? Luke's already thrown a lot of credit my way, even with Rachel Hartman. Her magazine is a national publication."

"Which also means that if he fails, he fails in the national spotlight and we'll be connected to that failure. We have to consider that."

Ruby had thought about it plenty, but not in the professional sense. "It'll kill him. Plain and simple. I don't think he'd ever recover from it, physically or emotionally."

"Are you sure you're ready to watch that happen?"

She considered the question for a moment, then looked Lana straight in the eye. "Am I ready to stand by and do nothing when I could prevent it? Hold back my gifts and talents just because the stakes are too high?"

"The stakes *are* high. Very high. As your mentor and partner, I just want to make sure you recognize that." Then, in true straight-talking-Lana fashion, she asked, "After all, you said you had some unconventional therapy you wanted to do with him."

Ruby felt her face flush. "Nothing like that." Then, with a laugh she added, "I think I'd slap him if he tried."

"I should hope so," Lana replied. "Sounds like you've owed that man a slap for six years if you ask me." Her face softened. "I'm just trying to look out for my friend, okay?"

"You don't have to worry about Luke Buckton," Ruby said as the image of Luke flashing a million-watt smile Rachel Hartman's way returned to mind. "Just when you think he might be a good guy, he'll always find a way to remind you otherwise."

"No offense, but I'll be spending my time praying for 'otherwise.'"

"Pray for him to recover. He deserves that much." The image of Luke slamming his fist against his leg back on the guesthouse porch refused to leave her mind. No matter what he'd done to her, he deserved a recovery if God chose to grant him one. Everybody deserved to recover. That belief was at the very core of what she did. The thing with Luke was just that his recovery had to be on a grand scale for him to truly heal in his mind and heart.

And she'd uncovered just the way to do that. "As for that unconventional therapy, let me tell you what I've got in mind for tomorrow's session, and don't say no until you hear me out the whole way."

Friday morning, Luke got out of Ruby's compact car to stand in, of all places, the Red Boots parking lot. "We should have taken my truck."

"It would have spoiled the surprise." She was nervous, different than the level of confidence she usually displayed lately. Still, the slightly jittery Ruby tugged his heart's memory back to the sweet, fade-into-the-woodwork girl he'd fallen for in high school.

He'd dated dozens—maybe even hundreds—of women since high school. Fallen for a few of them, too. But he'd only ever really loved Ruby Sheldon.

That was then. This was now. And right now, he didn't know what Ruby was up to when she told him she had some sort of nontraditional therapy in mind. It was 9:30 a.m. and Red Boots didn't serve breakfast, so "food" wasn't the answer.

"Let's go inside," Ruby said. She had a look in her eyes that set off a tiny alarm in his stomach. "The owner's waiting."

The owner? Ruby Sheldon wasn't the kind of person to be friends with the owner of a place like Red Boots. Luke had been here enough times to know what this place was like. Wild nights, loud music, and…

It struck him like a two-by-four to his bad knee. He stopped and stared at Ruby. "You're not."

She kept right on walking. "Of course not. You are."

He had to stand there for a moment, hands on his hips, taking in the massive revelation she'd just dished up to him. *Girl, I didn't think you had it in you.*

Red Boots had a mechanical bull.

Suddenly, Luke wasn't sure *he* had it in *him.* All that bravado, those claims, all that grit, and Ruby Sheldon just called his bluff. It sunk a new kind of rock in his stomach.

Ruby was standing at the door, holding it open. "Well, get on in here and let's see what you're made of." When he shot her a look, she rolled her eyes and said, "We're going to go so slow you could probably take a nap up there if that's what you're worried about."

Luke settled his hat. "I'm not worried about nothin'. It's the Red Boots toy bull, after all. My baby nephew could ride it." Big talk for a guy whose pulse had just doubled.

Just as Luke reached the door, a grisly old cowboy came out, handing the keys to Ruby. "I'll be back in an hour. Lock 'er up and leave the keys in the mailbox if you leave before then." As he walked past Luke, the man offered a big old wink and said, "Ride 'em, cowboy."

"We were never here," Ruby called.

"Who? I don't hear nobody," the man called over his shoulder as he walked toward his truck at the far end of the parking lot.

Ruby looked at Luke. "Much as I know you love an audience, I didn't think you'd want one for this."

A gush of reassurance warred with the spike of wariness in his chest. No one ever knew him like Ruby did. *Does*. To be so known brought out more emotions than he could sort through at the moment.

The Red Boots was a different place in empty daylight. Quiet, almost hollow. "Do you know how to work that thing?" he asked as they made their way to the back bar where Buster Boot had been a fixture for years.

"I got lessons from Tyler yesterday afternoon. I even rode it." It was the closest thing to cocky he'd ever heard from Ruby, complete with a "so there!" look as she set down her purse and snapped on the lights. Did she offer that last little detail knowing it would guarantee his compliance? No way could he walk out now, aware that she had ridden the robotic little monster.

Luke stood there for a moment, looking at Buster's cartoonish face, startled at the ball of ice in his stomach. He'd stared down uglier beasts three times its size, but the thing still unnerved him. He hated that Ruby saw his nerves—he'd never been able to hide anything from her, then or now—but then again he knew there wasn't anyone else he'd have in the room with him for this.

She stepped into the padded ring and motioned for Luke to join her. He did, a zing down his bad leg offering an odd commentary on the feat. Ruby put one hand on the bull's head and held out her other hand to Luke. Unsure what this was all about, he gave her his hand, which she placed onto hers on the bull.

Touching the thing somehow broke the momentary chokehold his fear had over him. And yet he wasn't touching it, he was touching Ruby's hand touching it. As if she were the bridge between them—and wasn't she?

"I'm going to pray." She announced it as if praying over mechanical bull therapy in an empty bar happened every day. When he stared at her in what he thought was well-founded shock, Ruby eyed him and said, "So pray with me."

What could he do? Even that Pastor Theo guy would find this a bit nuts. But Luke knew better than to argue with Ruby when she got that expression on her face. He shut his eyes.

"Father, You made all of us. You know us, our bodies, our abilities, our needs and fears. Lay Your hand on this machine and this man, see to it that Your will is done through our efforts both now and in the days to come. Amen."

Luke opened one eye. "Why'd you do that?"

She opened her eyes, but didn't move her hands from atop the bull and under his hands. "Why wouldn't I pray over something important?"

"'Cause it's *a mechanical bull*." He tried to keep the "isn't it obvious?" tone from his voice but didn't quite succeed.

"It's a mechanical bull that's about to show you what you can and cannot do yet. That's a big thing, and I always pray over big things. You might want to give it a try."

She'd always been able to wake up the spiritual side of him—what little of it existed back then—and inspire him with her easy, effortless relationship with the Almighty. It had never come quite so easy to him. Truth be told, it hadn't come at all in the last few years. Sure, there were the hospital bed pleas, but Luke didn't think desperation prayers really counted as authentic faith. Ruby's faith was as authentic as they came. Ellie had always been like that, Gran was absolutely like that, and Gunner had become like that. He was trying not to think that much about it, but lately it seemed as if God was showing up everywhere.

Still, Red Boots was the last place he expected to bump up against the hand of God in his life.

All this was slamming around his brain while Ruby just stood there, as if waiting for him to catch up to her. After a moment she said softly, "Get on."

"I'm scared." It jumped out of him, two escapee words from behind his usual bravado. It made him crazy that they had slipped out *to her*, revealing a run-and-hide impulse he'd never want anyone—especially not Ruby—to see.

"Of course you are." She didn't seem to think one bit less of him for admitting it. "I'm scared for you, too. Get on anyway."

It was that simple, wasn't it? For a crazy moment he wanted to pull her toward him and kiss her—from habit, or old love, or just stalling, he couldn't say which—but had enough wits about him to realize what a seriously stupid idea that was. Instead, he nodded and gave her hand a squeeze.

It was a dumb mechanical amusement ride in a building where nobody was watching. It should have been the easiest thing in the world. Instead, it felt as if he was taking the entire world on his shoulders as he threw his leg over the thing. He was maybe three feet off the ground, but his stomach did summersaults as if standing on the edge of a high cliff. He slipped his left hand into the braided rope handhold and felt his breaths come short and panicked. This was a hundred times more difficult than he'd imagined—and that wasn't even the physical challenge of it.

Help! he yelped silently from some place deep in his chest, and with a startle realized it was a prayer. He looked over Ruby as he settled himself a second time, her steady gaze an anchor in the nervous swirl all around him. Feeling like he was gulping down his last breath, Luke slid up on the rope and nodded.

Chapter Twelve

Ruby's heartbeats were galloping, her whole body thrumming with anxiety and purpose. She'd known from the moment the idea came to her that this was the first step Luke needed. She couldn't believe it when Lana actually agreed. Clinically, it would tell her where his balance was off and what muscles weren't working the way they ought to. Emotionally, it would show him—in a way he couldn't ignore—what he could and couldn't do.

All of that made great sense ten minutes ago. Right now, even with Lana's blessing, it felt like a huge risk. An absurdly unconventional therapy for a man unlike any she'd ever known.

A man she still cared for way more than she should.

Lana was right; there was no point in pretending this was any kind of conventional patient/therapist relationship. She couldn't classify this struggle they were in together—it was beyond physical, beyond emotional, partly spiritual, partly professional, and 100 percent confusing.

Stay close, Lord, guide my hand. Show both of us what we need to see, even if it's not what we want to see.

Pulling in a breath, Ruby turned the key in the controls. The machine gave a little rumble and a small lurch, startling both of them. Then it stilled, the only sound the hum of the mechanism waiting to move. She turned the dial.

With a grinding sound, the bull began to swerve comically slowly, ducking and raising its big brown head. At first, Luke's body stiffened, his eyes as wide as the false glassy orbs on the bull.

Ruby tamped down her heart—currently stuck in her throat for what she knew Luke was feeling—and forced her therapist self to kick in. Gradually, the instinctual counterbalance seemed to wake up in his spine. She wondered if he even knew his right hand had risen in the posture all riders adopted. She watched the left leg—was it sensing his body position, was it flexing and releasing with control? Would Luke's body, so finely trained to react in split-second timing, remember the skill it had been famous for?

She waited until he seemed impatient with the current pace before adjusting the dial. With a few hisses and whirrs, the bull picked up speed and made more exaggerated movements. She watched Luke's face take on the laser focus of an athlete, even though she could still read fear in his eyes. This was the equivalent of asking a thoroughbred jockey to ride a carousel pony—it wasn't a true match to his skills—but that didn't mean it wasn't a challenge. This new speed came slightly easier to him, however, since it was a bit closer to what he'd been used to. She watched his hips, watched the muscles in his back stretch and flex. Ruby felt a little light-headed and realized she'd been holding her breath. She let the machine go two whole minutes at this level before turning it up one notch.

The bull's movements became more jerky, the swings dipping lower and higher, direction changes coming one on top of the other. Luke's face hardened into gritted teeth, his eyes down on the shoulders of the mechanical monster, a tense face but a body swerving in an almost graceful way atop the frantic mass. They were still at only one-third the machine's possible levels, but he'd been riding for over six minutes now, and the room's colored lights showed sweat breaking out on his forehead. Ruby felt as if she were sweating herself.

At eight minutes, she turned the machine off, the mechanism slowing down until it came to a halt. Even from where she stood outside the padded ring, she could hear Luke's breath coming hard and fast.

It was a long moment before he looked up at her, his face an unreadable mix of pain, victory and doubt.

"Eight minutes, twenty seconds," she said, reading the digital time display on the control panel. She waited for the question he was going to ask, unsure how he would take the answer.

"What level?"

"Three."

Luke wiped his mouth with the back of his hand and muttered something she was sure she'd rather not hear. Then he looked up at her, eyes hard. "Three, huh? Felt like seven."

She didn't reply. He'd have to wrestle with this on his own. She waited for him to dismount. He didn't. Instead, he recentered himself on the bull. "Turn it on again."

"Luke…"

He flexed his fingers inside the handhold. "Turn it on again." She'd been foolish enough to think it wouldn't come to this. The only way Luke was going to get off that bull was by force—and not force of will. By force of gravity.

"You might hurt yourself." The warning hung useless in the air. She knew those eyes, knew that man. There was no reasoning with him when he got like this. Better to have him fall on the padding here than in the arena or in front of the cameras. If he was going to end his career by force, this was the least horrible place to do it. Her heart sagged at the prospect of having to bear witness to it. But her gift was bearing witness to pain, and this moment was of her own doing.

Her expression must have shown her feelings, for Luke caught her eyes and said "Just the next two levels. If I can."

Those last words were for her benefit— Luke never said "if I can" to any challenge. It was win or go down swinging. She honestly worried that if she didn't comply, Luke would come back here and press Tyler until he gave in—and that had no hope of ending well.

Stay close, Lord. Save him from himself, if that's Your will. I'll try to pick up the pieces as best I can. "One minute each level. No more." There was no point in arguing. Instead, she stared up at him until he stopped adjusting his position and met her gaze. "Be careful, Luke." It felt about as useless as asking a tidal wave to play nice, but she couldn't help herself.

She switched it on.

The first two levels went smoothly—well, smoothly by mechanical bull standards. By the third minute—the level he'd achieved last time—she began to hear grunts from him and his body looked less in control. The fourth minute, he looked as if he'd go airborne any second, his arms and legs closer to flailing than the deliberate counterbalance of a bull rider. Ruby felt her breath come in short spurts, her fingers clenching the dial while her eyes shifted from the timer to Luke and back again.

At fifteen seconds into the fifth minute, Luke's grip gave out and the bull threw him into the far side of the padded ring.

"Luke!" She slammed the controls to the off position as he rolled across the padding ending with his back to her. She saw his legs recoil, drawing up in what could only be pain. The whole thing had been a stupid mistake, an indulgence of his determination that never should have happened.

Ruby climbed over the railing to dash unsteadily across the thick padding as Luke rocked back and forth. He gave a moan, and her heart sunk. He'd set back his healing if not destroyed it all together, and she'd been the one who made it happen. "Luke! Are you hurt? In pain?" Silly questions to a man moaning on the ground. Ruby reached him, rolling him by the shoulder until he lay, eyes squeezed shut, face up.

He gave a tight moan, one hand clutching his left hip.

"Can you move? Did you hurt yourself?"

He still hadn't opened his eyes. Ruby's pulse was slamming up against her ribs.

"Ouch," he pushed out in more exhale than word. Then one eye opened. "But not as much ouch as I remember." A smile—a pained smile but a smile nonetheless—spread across his features.

Ruby whacked her hands against his chest. "You're not hurt!"

He winced a bit. "I didn't say that."

"You're not *really* hurt. You scared me to death."

His hands wrapped around her wrists and held her palms to his chest. "Aww, you care."

The look in his eyes toed up against an imaginary line they'd drawn between them.

"Of course I do." And then, just to cover the heat she felt rising up her back, she added, "I can't get a reputation for injuring my most famous patient, can I?"

She went to sit back, to put some space between them, but he kept his hold on her wrists. "Ruby…" Most of her wished he didn't say her name in the mesmerizing way he did.

"No, don't."

"Wait a minute. Please. Let me say this." With a grin, he added, "It'll give me a dignified way to catch my breath."

Catch *his* breath maybe. Ruby was currently finding it hard to breathe with the way Luke was looking at her. In all the risks of today's stunt, this was a danger she hadn't counted on facing.

"You knew. You knew I needed to do this, and *how* I needed to do this. No one's ever been able to figure me out like you have. It's why I knew I couldn't do this without you." One hand released her wrist to come up and brush his fingertips against her cheek.

For a moment she was back in high school, smitten and flabbergasted that such a touch could ever happen. How did this attraction still hold so much power after all that pain and all those years? Despite every logical reason to the contrary, Ruby couldn't say whether she'd resist if he chose to kiss her just now. He knew it—she could read it in his eyes.

She wanted to have something clever to say, some snappy comeback to put a safe lid on the box of fireworks Luke kept opening up between them. Instead, a potent and sizzling silence stretched between them. She considered giving in, letting him kiss her just to feel that thrill again. To remember what it was like when the dashing, popular boy had eyes only for her. When life wasn't tangled and full of pressures and the future had a million possibilities even in tiny Martins Gap.

Luke's hand slid from her cheek to the back of her neck. Any moment he would pull her face toward him and take them down that perilous road again.

Somewhere, way down deep below her galloping heart, she found the solid core of resistance, the scar still left from the pain. Ruby reached up and pulled his hand away. "Don't."

He released his grip on her. "Why?"

Now it was she who closed her eyes. "Because we're not those people anymore."

"I know that."

Did he, really? "Sit up, Luke. It's time to go. You did what we came here to do."

* * *

Luke and Gunner sat on the big house steps the next night, a box of Shorty's pizza open between them. It was something they hadn't done together in years—a throwback to the times when Luke was just Gunner's gawky kid brother. To the times when they were allies against the common enemy—their father's temper.

"Ugh. It's still as bad as it was back then," Luke said as the gooey cheese stretched off his bite.

"That's what so good about it." Gunner hoisted the tip of his own huge slice toward his mouth. "Junky, greasy—pizza isn't supposed to come any other way in my book."

"You need to get out more," Luke replied behind a mouthful of oily cheese and questionable pepperoni. "This is barely pizza by my standards."

"You could always go inside and make yourself a salad."

Luke laughed. "Not a chance."

"Beats going shopping with Gran and the girls for that bridal shower, that's for sure. Should we have invited cousin Witt?" Gran, Ellie, Brooke, Audie and baby Trey had gone into Austin to go shopping for a family bridal shower for Witt's upcoming wedding to Jana.

"Then we'd probably end up eating burgers."

"That's true. Hey, I did my interview with Ms. Hartman. She let it slip about some big upcoming event. I think it's time you let us in on what you've got planned. Ruby isn't talking, but I know she knows."

She knew all right, even if she wasn't happy about it. The exhibition ride was coming, even if they hadn't yet set a date. He'd made it to level five on that mechanical bull, and while he was sore, his knee hadn't buckled once today. His leg had held up reasonably well on Buster Boots, even if his reactions were sluggish and off. Maybe it was time to let the family know. They'd push back, for sure, but he was ready. "I'm gonna ride."

"Ride?"

Luke tried not to be annoyed at the look of utter disbelief on his brother's face. "An exhibition ride, not a competitive one."

"Come on, Luke, are you really ready? I mean, a horse is one thing, but a bull…"

"I know what I'm doing. I've got feeling back. It hurts, and it's weaker than I'd like, but I'll work with it. The longer I stay out, the harder it'll be to come back. You know how this works. The sponsors are getting itchy. An *exhibition* ride," he repeated, seeing Gunner's face still set in a doubtful frown. "No competition."

Gunner sat back, offering only a grunt. "You knew I was going back."

"That's not what you said back in the barn a few weeks ago. Back then it sounded like there was a possibility you might not ever go back."

"That was before I could feel my leg. Back before Ruby got it working again."

Gunner pulled one hand through his hair. "Yeah, and there's another thing. You're not looking to take up with her again, are you?"

"No." Even he didn't believe that answer. Back at Red Boots, so many of his old feelings for her had kicked into high gear. She was right, though—they were different people. Only the singular difference he'd noticed at that moment was that the old Luke wouldn't have respected her refusal, and would have charmed her into a kiss. And another. He knew how to push her buttons just as accurately as she know how to push his.

"Forgive me if you don't sound too convinced." Gunner evidently could read him better than Luke remembered. "There's a lot of water under the bridge between you two. Things could get messy." After a moment, Gunner added. "She deserves better than that."

"She deserves better than me, that's for

sure. Even if everything else weren't messed up between us, I'm not staying and she's not leaving."

"I'm glad you see that. But you know," Gunner flipped the box open again and grabbed another slice, "'not staying' could still include a few more visits. Gran's really happy you're here."

This was a topic Luke had actually meant to talk to Gunner about. "How is she? Really."

"She's pushing ninety—the years are catching up to her." Gunner sat back after taking an enormous bite. The man always could inhale a pizza. "She's slowing down— not that she'd admit it to anyone. That's where you get it from, you know."

"My admirable tenacity?"

Gunner bumped Luke's shoulder. "Your infuriating bullheadedness." Gunner's features changed. "She won't be here forever. Spend some real time with her while you can."

His brother's words pulled a sharp pain in Luke's gut. He and Gran locked horns so often when he was in high school, but he always knew she loved him. She'd been a fierce, unrelenting anchor for him back when he had precious few moorings in this world. He'd talked himself out of missing her so many times in those first few years away, calling to mind the disappointed face she'd held as he'd gotten on his motorcycle and driven away for the last time. Luke's charm enabled him to get away with a lot in the world, but charm never worked with Gran. He was just coming to realize what a gift that was. Up until the accident, his world was sorely short of folks who would shoot straight with him. "True friends," Gran would call them—right after she yelled at him for treating Ruby like anything but a "true friend, much less a true love."

Such pinches of regret didn't agree with him these days. "This from the guy who disappeared for how many years?" he defended. "Who didn't make it home for dad's funeral?" Gran's face when he'd left town had nothing on the way she'd looked when Gunner had missed Dad's funeral.

Gunner's face hardened. "You never could resist a low blow." He set down the pizza slice. "And it's not like I didn't deserve that. But I came back. And I stayed. Things are going good here. Don't keep away, that's all I'm saying. I don't want the next time you show up to be Gran's funeral."

The remark chilled him. "C'mon, she's all right, isn't she? I mean, you'd tell me if there was something serious going on, right? This is Gran, she'll go on forever."

"No one does, Luke. Look, I get why you left. And I'm glad you came back to get all this straightened out. But family, man, you've got to hang on to that. Look at you and Tess. She's your twin sister, you used to be so close, and now she's halfway around the world taking photos in Australia for that travel magazine she works for. She leads a pretty interesting life, you know. Or wouldn't you, since when's the last time you talked to her?"

If Gunner had to go looking for a subject more sore than Gran, he'd found it. His beef with Tess had started when he'd left and just grew from there. Never one to hold back on opinion, Tess made sure he knew how she felt—not just about bull riding, but about the rowdy nights and the strings of buckle bunnies, too. "I got tired of her riding me all the time. No one needs their twin sister to act like their mother, you know?"

"Maybe it's because she loves you and worries about you. Who enjoys their twin brother gaining a rep as rodeo's resident bad boy?"

Luke felt his back stiffen. "So that's it? Forget the championships, the prize money, the acclaim, y'all just can't see past the scandal sheets?" Everybody in this family was always trying to make him into someone he wasn't. Luke had never been "pillar of the community" material—that was Gunner's new role. Right here was a perfect example of why he needed to put Martins Gap in his rearview mirror back then—and maybe still today.

Luke got up, his leg throbbing and needing a stretch. "Look, I don't want to fight with you. This stuff's been going on for years. It's not gonna suddenly melt into happy family sunshine just because I fell off a bull."

Gunner managed a small smile. "A bull throws you ten feet in the air into a metal fence and you're gonna go with *fell*?" He shut the pizza box. "Call Tess. It would mean the world to Gran if you mended fences with her here before you…left. Whenever that is."

He could do that much for Gran. After all, he'd left things badly with his twin sister at Ellie's wedding. "Maybe."

"Thanks."

It struck him just then, turning to look at his older brother who'd striven to pull the Buckton family back together from its splintered quartet of siblings, had even brought Witt from the estranged branch of Bucktons into the fold. "You're better than him, you know."

"Than who?"

"Than Dad. This 'head of the family' thing. The ranch, us. You handle it better than him. Just saying."

The smile that crossed Gunner's face was a full, true grin. "A compliment. From my little brother. Just how hard did your head hit that fence?"

Gunner was rewarded with a clod of dirt kicked over his boots. By Luke's bad leg. Which wasn't so bad anymore after all.

Chapter Thirteen

It was hard to see Luke again. He'd ruffled her composure so much back at the Red Boots, she wasn't quite sure how she'd feel at his next therapy appointment. Today she wished his training was at the medical center, not the Blue Thorn where so many memories lurked.

"Good morning, sunshine." Luke, ever the showman, didn't look the slightest bit fazed when he met her at the guesthouse door. She knew better than to believe the facade—the connection they'd almost reforged at Red Boots was as strong for him as it was for her. He was just infinitely better at keeping it hidden. It gave him a decidedly unfair advantage.

She hugged her files like a shield. "Good morning to you, too. How's the leg feeling?"

"Feeling," he smirked. "And that's a good thing. Glad to be hurting, you know?"

That was a dangerous subtlety. Neuropathy or paralysis patients often struggled with feeling whole again, and could turn pain—or the pursuit of it—into an obsession. The "if I hurt then I'm alive" mentality could take some people down a dangerous path. "You need to take this at a reasonable speed. Do you think you can do that, mister 'let's go two more levels until I'm thrown off'?"

"Hey," he countered. "The whole thing was your idea. You had to know I'd do that."

She had. She had known full well he'd run the risk of going beyond his abilities yesterday. Letting him go up to level five had been a calculated risk. He would have found a way to do it anyway. At least Red Boots was a controlled environment. Rodeo arenas weren't padded; no bucking bull had an "off" switch. "Are you ready to work? I've come up with some new regimens now that we know how your leg behaves." When Luke gave a "this ought to be fun" smirk, she cautioned, "This will hurt."

He spread his hands wide. "Bring it on."

Twenty minutes later, as sweat beaded off his forehead and grunts punctuated his every move, Luke lost his zeal. "You weren't kidding."

He was much easier to handle while he was

taxed. He didn't have enough energy to flirt, so they could keep to the task at hand. He waited until she announced the final set of exercises before mentioning, "Rachel is going to come watch Friday's session."

"Oh really? Quick left. Did it occur to you to ask me if this was okay by me? Right." She'd been calling out sudden direction changes while he paced around the room, rebuilding his reflexes and muscle memory. "Backward, now slow to the right. Three more minutes."

He stopped, pointing at her. "You're punishing me," he puffed, out of breath. It wasn't a whine, it was a declaration.

"I'm *treating* you. Quick right. I'm sorry if it feels like punishment, but you're the one who set the ambitious goal on the tight timeframe. Slow left."

"It's not the exercises, darlin', it's the attitude. You *want* me to hurt." He'd stopped just short of saying "you want to hurt me," but they both heard it in his voice.

She took the bull by the horns. "I do not want to hurt you. Left."

He stopped again. "You should. I hurt you."

He'd never admitted it so directly before. Yes, they'd had conversations that danced around how they were "different people" or "had history" but it had never come to admitting hurt. It took Ruby a moment to decide how to respond.

"Yes, you did." In for a penny, in for a pound. "You hurt me deeply, Luke Buckton."

Luke stopped walking, holding her gaze for a moment. His blue eyes looked like the depths went on forever. "I know that."

"Did you know it when you left? Did you think about it at all?" The distinction became suddenly important—only which was worse? To be deliberately hurt or just be the fallout of thoughtlessness? "Be honest. You owe me that much."

She was glad he paused and thought about it. "I wouldn't let myself think about it at first. I let all the dreams and the money dangling in front of my face crowd it out. I told myself Martins Gap couldn't hold me and it was—I don't know, my destiny or some such highfalutin thought—to leave."

He wasn't all wrong. Martins Gap couldn't hold him. "So you left Martins Gap." She found her courage and added, "And you left me."

"Yes." He regretted it. She was glad to see that much in his eyes.

She couldn't look at him, so she sorted through the pile of colored exercise bands sitting on the table. "You said such…hurtful things."

She heard him sigh. "I needed to burn the bridges behind me, I suppose. I figured we'd both be better off if you hated me."

Part of her had known he was acting out, even then, but that did little to dull the sting. "It doesn't work that way, Luke. When you love someone and you hurt them like that, all you do is make pain. You don't flip some switch and turn love to hate."

"I don't know. It worked with my dad. I sure hated him by the end."

It surprised her that she couldn't really refute that. Gunner Buckton Sr. had indeed managed to flip that switch. As far as she knew, he'd been a decent enough father when his wife was still alive—stern, but loving in his own brusque way. That had changed when he became a widower, and by the end his children hated him. Knowing Granny B the way she did, it had always amazed her how a man raised by someone so loving could be so skilled at raising hate in his children. It made a sick sort of sense, now that she thought about it. Luke's life had taught him that if you said enough hurtful things, hate grew. Only Ruby was pretty sure all that business between Luke and Gunner Sr. was about pain rather than hate.

"So did you hate me, in the end? Do you hate me now?"

That felt like an absurd question, given how much time she'd spent with Luke since his return to town. "I couldn't be this nice to you if I hated you now."

He laughed, but not out of humor. "Yeah, you could. You're that good of a person. And that's not an answer."

The answer should be easy, but it wasn't. He was asking what she felt for him, and the truth was she felt so many things for him it defied a simple answer. She opted for honesty. "No, I don't hate you. I hate how you hurt me, but that's not the same thing."

Luke leaned up against the wall, bad leg crossed over good with most of his weight on the good leg. He stuffed his hands in his pockets. "So what are we, then?"

"Patient and therapist."

Now he genuinely laughed. "Nope. Well, yes, but not just."

High school sweethearts. Old loves. Friends. Exes. None and all of the above. She shrugged. "I don't know what we are."

"I wanted to kiss you back at Red Boots. I

would have, if you'd let me." That was Luke—direct as a missile and just as explosive.

"I know." It wasn't much of an answer, but her insides were tumbling in every direction.

"Kissing you was always so…amazing. Still would be, I think."

"That's the problem, isn't it? There's this thing between us. Like fireplace embers. We could build it back up to flames in a second."

"We could."

"And it wouldn't change anything. It'd be nostalgia, Luke. Playing off something that *was* and pretending it's something that still *is*. And it'd feel great—for a moment. And then you'll leave and I'll stay. Don't you think one round of that kind of hurt is enough?"

"So then what? I don't want to put some silly box around what we are. I used to think we had to be an all-or-nothing thing, but I don't think that's true anymore. Can't we just make it up as we go from here?"

"So you can kiss me and still leave?"

"No. Well, okay, maybe. I mean, come on, who doesn't like a spectacular kiss? If you were some other girl, maybe I'd try for that. But that'd never be okay with you, I know that. I'm not that much of a jerk—well not anymore, anyway."

Ruby gathered up the bands from the table. "I think we're done here."

He pushed off the wall and leaned over to gather up the pile of bands he'd left on the floor. As he handed them to her, he said, "I like this between us—whatever this is. I meant what I said. I need you. If I'm going to pull this off, I've got to have you doing it with me. It's why I came home."

Why could he always pick the thing to say that dug deep into her heart? "You came for Gran," she countered.

"I thought I did, and I love her, but I figured out pretty quick that I really came for you."

"What am I supposed to do with a remark like that?"

"Come back on Friday and help me show the world what I can do."

Luke walked into the guesthouse and tossed the pile of papers on the table. It had been weird helping Gran sort through some of his old papers. He'd never been much for nostalgia, but she was getting a kick out of sifting through brittle old newspaper clippings from his high school days. She'd smile and put her hand to her chest when looking at photos of him as a toothy-grinned boy. She'd tsk and shake her head at shots of him as a wild, mussy-haired teenager.

She kept trying to foist a whole stack of things on him to keep, but he ended up packing most of it up into boxes and setting aside just a small pile for himself. Several were photos of him and Ruby during their inseparable days. Dreamy-eyed teenagers swimming in love. Had life ever really been that simple? Or were they just too young to see the complications?

Luke turned over his cell phone to see three missed calls from Nolan.

Nolan had called him? Not once but three times? Luke's heart kicked against his ribs at the prospect of good news from his agent. Nolan wouldn't be so insistent at delivering bad news—this had to be a welcome development, whatever it was.

He settled himself at the table, tilting the chair against the wall as he rubbed his hip. It ached something fierce after all the bending and reaching to fetch things down off the bookcases. He hated this old-man, creaky feeling. The numbness had always felt like a form of mental torture, but the constant nagging pain proved a new torment. It chipped away at his energy. Would it get better with more exercise? Or was this the way he'd feel from here on in? A young man dragging himself around in an old man's body?

Luke put it out of his mind and dialed, glad to hear Nolan pick up on the second ring. "Hey there, Luke," came Nolan's friendly voice. "How's it going down there on the family ranch?"

"It's going fine, Nolan. Healing fast. That reporter Rachel seemed charmed by the bison—and, of course, by yours truly. She's coming back tomorrow to interview Gran and Ellie and watch my session with Ruby. We want to make sure she has lots of good material to write me up nice."

"You always did know how to woo the press, Luke." There was a short pause. "That's why I know you'll be okay."

Luke caught the hesitation in Nolan's voice. "Why *wouldn't* I be okay?" When Nolan didn't come back with an immediate answer, Luke's gut sunk. "Whoa, Nolan. What's up?"

The sigh on the opposite end of the line dropped Luke's gut right down to the floor. "It's Tornado Tires."

Luke settled the chair back on the ground, his free hand on his forehead. Tornado had been with him for two years, and Nolan had been grooming them to be Luke's major sponsor. Luke had endured a mess of fancy dinners playing nice to Tornado's top brass. That couldn't go south now.

"They...well, the truth is that they pulled out this morning."

Luke pinched the bridge of his nose. He'd expected some of the smaller sponsors to get skittish, but not Tornado. "It's the middle of the season. They can't pull out. They always sponsor one of the top three riders."

"They've had a slow year. They need the visibility."

"How will they get visibility if they disappear off the sponsor roll?" He let his head fall back against the wall as he came up with the answer to his own question. "Tell me they didn't shift to Ray Knight. They can't do that in the middle of the season, can they?"

"Your contract has a 'no ride' clause letting them leave if you're out of the running for more than thirty days."

Luke stood up—too fast, sending zings down the back of his leg. "But I'm coming back. They know that."

There was a nasty pause before Nolan said "*We* know you're coming back."

"What's that supposed to mean?"

"*I* know you're coming back, and *you* know

you're coming back, but everyone else…well, they're not…convinced."

"What am I paying you for?" Luke began pacing the room. "Convince them. Send out a stack of press releases or reports or whatever it is y'all do up there."

"They carried you out of the arena on a stretcher, Luke. It's not like I can just make that go away. You know how this works. The press is like an animal. Unless you feed it, it goes hunting somewhere else."

"Rachel Hartman is here. I'm handing her every bit of detail I can, Nolan."

"We have to give her the one detail she wants. The one they all want. And I'm not sure how much longer they're going to wait for it. Set a date for your comeback ride, Luke. On JetPak. Give me a date, and I'll set every wheel in motion that I can."

Stay in the game. Feed the beast. He had no basis by which to set a date, but that couldn't matter right now. If he wanted to keep his career alive then he needed to give the media machine what it needed, and that was a date. And a rematch with JetPak. Whether or not it was wise? Well, that had to go by the wayside.

Luke stared at the Pro Tour schedule pinned to his wall. With a half sinking, half soaring feeling, he said "San Antonio. September in San Antonio."

"You're sure?"

Of course he wasn't sure. That was the whole point here, wasn't it? Well, Nolan always used to say that sometimes his job was to get from Luke just a bit more than he was ready to give. "Absolutely. Book it."

"Good thing. Glad to have you back, kid. I'll call you when I've set the details."

Luke ignored the hum of anxiety that just set up camp under his ribs. He wasn't "back," but he was on his way back, and that's what mattered.

He put down the phone, right next to a sweet photo of him and Ruby on prom night. He remembered feeling like he'd just seen the most beautiful girl on earth when she came out to meet him that night. She'd looked like a princess.

Ruby would get him on JetPak by September.

Only…would she? It was more likely Ruby would be furious at what he'd just done. She'd push for caution. She'd say he couldn't predict when he'd be ready. But she didn't understand the rules in play here, what he could lose if he stayed out of the spotlight for too long.

He couldn't do this without her, so he'd have to make her understand. Or at the very least, not get in his way.

Chapter Fourteen

Ruby sat opposite Luke and Rachel Hartman Friday morning at the picnic table in front of the ranch house. The reporter spread a file and a notebook open in front of her, a digital recording device set on the table between the three of them. The little red light blinked, a constant reminder that anything Ruby said would be "on the record."

According to Luke, Rachel had spent the last hour interviewing Gran. Now it was Ruby's turn. They'd spend thirty minutes talking, and then Rachel was going to observe Luke's therapy session. Ruby had no real reason to feel nervous—she knew she was simply a supporting player in this story—but anxiety tightened her stomach nonetheless.

"So what do you think of your star client?"

Rachel asked, pen poised over a fresh sheet of paper.

People around Martins Gap asked her that all the time. Those who knew their history added a wink and a nudge, those who didn't usually wanted to know what Martins Gap's most famous son was really like. She gave her now-standard reply. "He's a handful."

"A handful, with some pretty big goals. His comeback will be the story of the season. How does it feel to be at the center of it?"

That made Ruby laugh. She was never at the center of anything involving Luke Buckton. "Center? Not exactly."

"She's making it possible, though." Luke interjected. "I've made huge strides in my healing since I've been working with Ruby. I could have gotten treatment from anybody, but I chose to come home and get treatment from the person I trust most."

Ruby didn't doubt Luke felt that way, but this was a part of him she'd never liked. The "lay it on thick" Luke who came out once the cameras—or tape recorders—turned on.

Rachel looked at her. "He pays you quite a compliment." The reporter's smile widened. "Ellie tells me you two have a bit of history."

It annoyed Ruby that she felt heat rise in her cheeks. It was foolish to think she could get through this interview without her past relationship with Luke coming up, but she had hoped to get at least past the first five questions. "That was a long time ago. Yes we have 'a bit of history' as you put it, but it mostly means I know him well enough to work well with him. If that gives me an advantage to help him restore the function of his leg, then I'm glad for it."

Rachel circled something on her notepad. "So, old flame helps our star meet his new challenge, huh?"

Why had she let Luke talk her into this? "No, not exactly. My goal is functionality. What Luke does with that functionality is his own choice."

"So you don't endorse the exhibition ride on JetPak in September?"

Ruby shot Luke a look. They'd talked about the idea in vague terms but he hadn't mentioned that he'd set a date. In two months? On JetPak? And announced it to the press?

"I hadn't shared our announcement with Miss Sheldon yet, Rachel."

It dug under Ruby's skin that Luke called her "Miss Sheldon" while referring to the reporter as "Rachel." She scrambled for an appropriate response before settling on, "Well, this wouldn't be the first time I've seen Luke set a high bar for himself." The date teetered on the verge of reckless. Was he ever planning to ask her advice on the matter? Or was it just her job to get him to whatever date he chose?

Rachel clearly picked up on the tension. "What do you think of the idea?"

It was tempting to shoot Luke down for his arrogance in front of the press, but she wouldn't. "It'll be a ride worth watching, that's for sure." She was proud of her response. Truth, but enough of a dodge to keep her out of trouble. Luke's smile—half pleased, half "oops, maybe I should have told you that"—told her he felt the same. Luke may love this public relations game, but she found it exhausting.

Luke stood up. "How about we get to letting you see why that ride will be worth watching." As if to prove his point, he slid out of the picnic bench with an athletic grace she wouldn't have deemed possible weeks ago. He extended the bad leg out in front of him, wiggling the ankle back and forth. "See that? Now that's what I call functionality."

It was hard to call what they did next a true therapy session. To Ruby, it felt more like a show put on for Rachel's benefit. If he found any of his exercises taxing or painful, he hid it well. In fact, to the untrained eye, he gave a convincing exhibition of restored health. She didn't know whether to be impressed or angry. *He'll hurt after this*, she told herself. *More than usual thanks to overdoing it for show. Well, good. The pain might teach him a thing or two. Then again*, she thought, *he's an expert at ignoring all kinds of pain.*

"I don't suppose it'll surprise you to hear there's been some doubt as to whether or not you can do this," Rachel added when Luke finished one of his exercises with a dramatic flourish.

"Which is exactly why you're here. I *can* do this. I could announce it twelve ways to Sunday, but it's much better if you do. Show the world. Maybe you should add some video. Can you get a camera crew?"

Ruby wanted to roll her eyes. Did he ever stop? She could just imagine the havoc a television crew would wreak on tiny little Martins Gap. If he wanted to launch a media circus, he should be in Austin, not inflicting his spotlight on everyone here.

Thankfully, Rachel didn't seem interested. "I work for a magazine, Luke. We'll get some photographs later and the day of the event, but I'll leave the video to someone else."

"Your loss." Luke set down the kettle ball he'd been holding during a series of lunges.

"I think I'll live," Rachel replied.

"That's our last set of reps," Ruby announced, ready to end this little dog and pony show. She turned to Rachel. "Do you have any more questions for me?"

Rachel held out her hand. "No, I think I'm good. Thanks for your time and for letting me observe. I have a lot of respect for physical therapists—my father had a bad accident and he can still walk because of some great therapists like you."

She's nice, Ruby chided herself. *She's just doing her job. It's Luke you should be mad at, springing that on you the way he did.* As Rachel gathered up her notebook and headed to her car, Ruby changed her mind. *No, you should be mad at yourself. For expecting Luke to act like anyone but Luke. This is who he is, who he's always been.*

The moment Rachel was out of sight, Ruby turned to Luke. "September? You told them you'd ride JetPak only two months from now? What happened to 'well, maybe not the meanest bull'? What were you thinking?"

"One of my biggest sponsors ended our contract yesterday, and another one is talking about pulling out. We had to give them something or I'll have no sponsors left."

He made it sound like the end of the world. "Sponsors. You'll risk your body— your health, how you'll walk the rest of your life—based on a sponsorship budget? Do you understand, Luke, I mean *really* understand, what could happen if you do this too soon?"

"I know what will happen if I don't do it soon enough." He went to grab her hand and she dodged away from him, grabbing at her files instead and stuffing them angrily back into her bag. "Look, I know I should have told you before Rachel let it slip. I goofed there. But we had to get the word out to the press as soon as possible and she was coming today."

She turned to him. "And there are no phones in Martins Gap? Your laptop doesn't work well enough for you to send me an email? You don't know where I live?" She didn't wait for him to concoct an answer. "No, you knew exactly what I'd say to a scheme like that so you didn't bother to tell me. 'Oh Ruby, I need you,' 'Oh Ruby, I can't do this without you.' You expect me to believe it when you do something like this?"

He scoffed. "Hey, this is *my* career we're talking about."

"No. You're wrong, Luke. This is your

life we're talking about. I wonder, now, if you even know the difference? This is about what happens when you're forty, and fifty and sixty. After the cameras are turned off and you've left the arena and have to live the rest of your life with whatever injuries you've taken."

He waved her words away. "I can't think about that now."

She wanted to shake him. "You *have* to think about that now. I can't understand why you think bull riding is all there is. This won't last your whole life. This is one piece of it, and you're willing to throw everything all away just to hang on." She made herself say: "when maybe you're going to have to let go."

Luke stood very still, staring at her as if she'd just pulled his heart out of his chest. Maybe she had.

Maybe he needed to know what that felt like.

Luke watched as Ruby stormed across the lawn to haul off down the drive in a cloud of dust.

That hadn't gone the way he'd planned.

At least she'd pitched her fit after Rachel left. Admittedly, he'd done that on purpose, let her find out in front of Rachel, knowing she wouldn't throw him under the bus in front of the press. Okay, he didn't feel so great about that, but if this wasn't the time to take bold steps, he didn't know what was.

He looked up to see Gran scowling at him from the big house steps. She must have seen the way Ruby left. She made her way down to him, and he braced for whatever was coming. "What have you done now?"

He told her what he'd done and why, ready to just get the coming lecture over with. Instead, she just closed her eyes and sighed. Luke hated when she did that—Gran angry was always easier to deal with than Gran quietly enduring her disappointment.

"I had to get her to go along with it, Gran."

"And you think you've done that? You haven't. You've manipulated her, and you know it. What's the matter with you, son? You tell me you need her and yet you treat her like that? That's not how we should treat people who are important to us—" she leveled her worst glare at him "—people we care about. Where is this changed man you keep telling me you are? I'm not seeing him, Luke. Not at all."

"She'd have said no if I'd asked, and I can't get a 'no' now, Gran. I can't."

She waved his justification away as if it

were a pesky fly. "No, you just want to get your way. Always have. Only sometimes getting your way isn't worth the cost you have to pay to get it."

He started to walk away, figuring her lecture was over. It wasn't. "Do you still have that Bible?" she called after him.

He stopped, his own eyes closed. "Yes, ma'am."

"Genesis. Won't be hard to find, boy, it's the first book."

"I know that, Gran."

"Jacob. You remember what I used to call him, don't you?" With that, she turned and walked back into the house. Out of some foggy cloud of memory, the story of Jacob bubbled up. Jacob the trickster, Gran had always called him. How many times had she compared Luke and Gunner to Jacob and Esau—even though Luke was twins with Tess, not Gunner.

Luke didn't often do what he was told—most especially with commanded Bible readings—but for some reason he couldn't stop himself from flipping through the first part of the book until he found the heading "Jacob and Esau" and began reading.

Chapter Fifteen

Ruby turned the key in her door Sunday afternoon, Oscar tugging hard on his leash for his weekly romp in the park between church and supper at Mama's house. He began barking furiously, and Ruby turned to find Luke standing on the sidewalk with a picnic basket in his hands.

"You cancelled on me."

She had. She'd never done that before, but even Lana okayed the tactic. Ruby was angry and confused and in no fit state to work with him. Luke needed to realize there were consequences to treating a therapist like some kind of adjunct to his public relations campaign. And, quite frankly, she needed time to decide what to do next.

"You didn't answer my calls yesterday," he said, shrugging with one hand in his pocket.

"Your mom said you usually took your dog for a walk on Sunday afternoons. You've got a dog?"

"You sound like you're surprised." She stood there while Oscar rushed up to Luke, jumping up against Luke's shins to sniff at the basket. Usually Ruby trusted Oscar's instincts where people were concerned, but clearly whatever was inside that bright blue gingham cloth had charmed the mutt out of his good dog sense.

"I pegged you for a cat person, actually. You never really cared for Brick." With one hand he flipped open one end of the picnic basket and reached inside to produce a sizable bone-shaped dog biscuit. Oscar dissolved into a frenzy of excitement. *He's cheating. Be smarter than that, Oscar. He's just bribing you. He bribes everyone—or at least he thinks he does.*

Oscar paid no mind to her silent advice. "Well," Ruby replied, frowning at her pushover of a dog, "Brick was a disaster on four legs." She called an image to mind of the scrappy, disobedient, reddish-brown dog that considered the entire world his chew toy. Luke was right—she'd tried hard to like that dog and failed. His habit of stealing and shredding her shoes made it nearly impossible. Luke—a fellow rebel—had loved him, of course.

Luke raised up the basket like a peace offering. "Can we talk?" He produced a second dog biscuit, tossing it into Oscar's eager mouth. *Traitor.*

"I'm not sure what there is to talk about." She started walking toward the park, not willing to surrender a perfectly good Sunday to the Luke Buckton "I Want My Way" campaign. No matter what smelled so delicious in that basket.

He fell into step beside her. "Come on, Gran helped me make this. Let's have a picnic like we used to and see if we can't figure out how to make this work."

She wished she didn't notice how smooth his gait had become. He really had made remarkable progress—but that and nostalgic picnics didn't pave the way for the absurd thing he had already set in motion. "Well picnic or not, you're off to a poor start. Shoving a timeframe down my throat in front of a reporter is no way to gain my cooperation."

"That was a bad move, I admit. I boxed you into a corner to get my way. That isn't the way I should treat you."

She didn't reply, but kept walking. At least he'd admitted what a conniving thing he'd done. She wasn't entirely sure, however, that this picnic wasn't just more conniving.

"I get that this isn't how you'd do it if you had a choice. But I need you to get that *I* don't really have a choice, either."

That stopped her. "I don't believe that. You do have a choice. And you made a bad one."

He stopped walking, turning to look at her. "I'm not ready to leave the rodeo, Ruby. I will be someday. I know it's not my whole life. But my exit has got to be done the right way. How I leave determines what I can and can't do afterward. I need to leave on my terms. It's going to be *me* calling the shots on my last ride, not the rodeo leaving me behind."

She resumed walking. "And you think riding JetPak when you're not fully healed will do that."

"That hunk of US prime beef does not get the last word on my career. I won't give that to him. Or at the very least, I won't walk away knowing I just *handed* it to him. If he gets it, it'll be because we fought and he won."

She didn't like the way he was thinking about this. Hadn't that bull already won? "And what happens if he tosses you a second time? Will it just become about going a third round?"

"It's not going to come to that."

He sounded all too certain. "How do you know?"

"I've gone eight seconds on JetPak twice before. That last ride was a fluke—a mistake on my part because Ray Knight got into my head and rattled me. That will never happen again."

She hadn't known that. Well, of course she hadn't known that—Luke wouldn't openly admit a weakness. She'd always assumed that Luke simply found the bull he couldn't ride. It hadn't really occurred to her that maybe that fateful ride had been more about Luke *losing* than about JetPak *winning*. It certainly explained his thinking. "You never told me that."

"You never asked. You've never asked me about that ride at all."

She looked at him as they turned the corner into the little fenced-in park where she loved to let Oscar run free. "You told me you didn't remember the accident."

"I don't remember what happened *after* the accident, no. But I remember every detail of that ride. I knew exactly how I let Ray get to me, how I let him mess with my focus. I could tell you exactly what mistake I made and when. To be honest, I think it'd be easier if I didn't remember it, but then there'd be all that videotape to remind me."

It explained his massive levels of frustration and impatience. It was *he* who defeated himself that day, not JetPak. No wonder a rematch meant so much to him. She knew that Luke had probably worked out precisely how to correct his errors. The only thing left was retraining his body to comply.

Luke pulled a turquoise-checked tablecloth from the picnic basket and spread it on a soft patch of ground under the shade of a live oak. "So," he said as he lowered himself down on the ground with a fair amount of ease and only a little grunt, "I know what happened. I know why. It wasn't lack of ability that sent me sailing into that railing, it was lack of focus. I dropped my guard for a moment and paid the price. Now I want it back." The words came hard, his eyes fierce. Ruby was staring right into the truth that kept him up nights, the misstep that served as the ground zero of his bitter impatience. It was an immovable path he was on, one from which he could not stray and live with himself.

She was glad when Oscar began to nose his way into the basket—the moment needed a bit of comic relief. "Hey there, buddy," Luke laughed, "you already got yours. These are for us." He grinned at her as she settled opposite him on the cloth. "I went all out. All your favorites."

He had way too much ammunition to wage his campaign. "Gran's brownies, of course, but that's for later—unless you want to ditch convention and eat dessert first. But I know how much you loved Gran's buttermilk fried chicken." He waggled his eyebrows playfully as he pulled out a container of the savory dish.

"That's not fair," she said as the aroma washed over her. Lots of Texans were passionate about their barbecue, but to Ruby it had always been about the fried chicken. And no one made fried chicken like Gran. Ruby could have just eaten a twelve course meal and the smell of Granny B's chicken could still make her hungry. "You know how I feel about Granny B's fried chicken."

Luke grinned. "I was counting on that. Oh, and what's chicken without..." He unfolded a napkin to reveal a half dozen biscuits.

Some women loved ice cream or chocolate. Ruby loved biscuits. Warm with honey butter or jam or smothered in gravy, biscuits were her comfort food. It was a red-letter day the afternoon Granny B trusted her with the Buckton family biscuit recipe. They'd been sitting on her front steps with a handful of biscuits stolen from Granny B's kitchen when Luke had told her he loved her for the first time.

She hadn't made them in years, feeling as if Luke's departure severed her from the Buckton family and the rights to that recipe.

Ruby stared at the display, the memories, emotions, and scents combining to overwhelm her. She felt out of control in the best and worst ways. "You really did go all out," she gushed, unsettled by how smitten he could make her feel. It was a talent of his—pulling out all the stops to get what he wanted. He could do it to lots of people, to a degree. Unfortunately, he knew her well enough to be render her nearly helpless at the moment.

"I need you, Ruby. I need you enough to make me pull something stupid like revealing the news at the interview with Rachel. I'll keep saying it until you believe me because you can get me there. JetPak took a lot from me, but I can win it back. If you help me."

She wanted to believe him. She understood how he needed to regain what he'd felt he lost. It didn't make sense—it was still a monumental risk—but things like this didn't always make sense. This was a final, essential showdown to Luke, and he would never let this go. He'd come back at it until he came out on top—only each round of the showdown would cost Luke more.

The smart thing to do would be to walk away from his irresponsible obsession, to remove herself from the situation. Even Lana had suggested it—again.

Only she couldn't. And not because of the picnic in front of her. This was Luke. And he was right: he needed her. She doubted anyone else would be able to get from him what was needed to meet this challenge. She couldn't shake the notion that to walk away now would be tantamount to the same abandonment he'd done to her, and she wasn't that kind of person. Crazy as it sounded, Luke's ride was a showdown of sorts for her as well; a way to leave this relationship behind on her terms rather than his.

Luke held her gaze. "I'm sorry. And I'll change. No more stunts, no more timeframes shoved down your throat. From now on, you'll call the shots on my treatment. Get me there, Ruby. Get me back on JetPak so I can have the rest of my life."

Ruby gave him a disbelieving look. "Luke Buckton, there isn't enough chicken and biscuits in the world to make me think you'll keep a promise to do what you're told."

She wasn't wrong. He was known for many things, but ready compliance had never been one of them. But if that was the price he had to pay to make this work, he'd pay it…even if it would chafe him. A lot. "I will. Do as I'm told, I mean." He pulled a plate from inside the picnic basket and handed it to her.

"You won't." She took the plate from him, giving him a skeptical look.

This was going to take some work. He'd expected it, and had a plan. "Test me."

She laughed at that as she added chicken, two biscuits, and a brownie to her plate. "How can I test something like that?"

"Tell me to do something—anything—and I'll do it."

He heaped his own plate while he let her think. When she finally made up her mind, she surprised him. "Sing."

Yeah right, he thought as he bit into a breast of chicken, *wouldn't that be funny?* He'd left her all the drumsticks, knowing they were her favorite. "You know I can't," he said with his mouth full.

One corner of her mouth turned up in a way that made him nervous. "Sing anyway," she said. "Stand up right here and sing the

Martins Gap Mustangs fight song. At the top of your voice." When he balked, she added, "I'm not kidding."

She wasn't. She'd called his bluff. This was a whole new Ruby, and he was coming to realize his old tactics were likely to turn on him—and just had. He stared at her for a second, then put his plate down. "You aren't kidding, are you?" He scratched his head, stalling until he could think of a way out of this one. "I'm not sure I remember the words."

"Hail the Mustangs, fear the Mustangs..." she cued, singing the first line of the song that echoed through every high school pep rally. Of course he knew the words. They'd be burned into his brain forever—and she probably knew that.

"Fall to the stampede," he finished soft and off-key, hoping that would suffice.

It didn't. "See? Comes right back to you, like riding a bicycle," she said, pointing at him. "Up. Now. And loud." When he hesitated, she gave him a glare worthy of a Sunday school teacher. "You said you'd do anything."

Luke shook his head, then bit back an unsavory exclamation as he pulled himself to a standing position. He could do it with ease now, but it still hurt. Oscar, the excitable little mutt who was supposed to be helping him win Ruby's partnership, began yapping at his feet until Ruby commanded him to sit in her lap as part of the "audience."

He looked around to see who was within regretful earshot, counting six poor souls who ought to be warned of what was coming. Ellie always said he couldn't carry a tune in a bucket, and she was right. This was going to be humiliating.

Humiliating, but worth it. Luke took a deep breath and launched into a loud, off-pitch rendition of the Martins Gap Mustangs fight song. Even Ruby cringed as she laughed, and an older couple at the edge of the park stared and pointed.

Might as well make the best of it. Luke began strutting, conducting an imaginary marching band, compensating for his lack of musical talent with rampant enthusiasm and sheer gutsy volume. When he finished the first verse, he went right on into the second. Oscar actually began howling along. He was glad to see tears in Ruby's eyes from laughing so hard. Making Ruby laugh had been his second favorite thing back in the day.

Making Ruby sigh had been the first. She

could sigh at him in a way that made him feel King of the World.

His task completed, Luke crumpled down to lie flat on his back on the blanket as Ruby, and even a few of the puzzled spectators, broke into applause. He laughed himself, one hand over his face, as amused as he was mortified. "See what I mean? Nobody can push me to extremes like you can."

"Oh," she said in a tone he'd never heard from her before, "you're not done."

Startled, he uncovered his eyes and rolled his head to look at her. "There are only two verses."

Ruby finished her drumstick and licked her fingers victoriously—really, that was the only way to describe it. "That was a test."

Not *the* test, *a* test. He didn't like what it implied.

"Now I have the real demand."

Luke looked at Oscar, who was staring at him from Ruby's lap with "now you're in for it" eyes. "Ouch," he told the dog. "I think I'm about to regret this, Oscar."

Ruby sat back on her hands and stretched out one foot to cross it over the other. "Church," she pronounced. "Every Sunday between now and the ride."

Luke felt as if someone had whacked him in the chest. "What'd Gran say to you?"

"Not a thing. This is my idea."

That was hard to believe. Gran had been on him to go to church from the minute he set foot back on Blue Thorn land. She kept going on about how he "needed to get his soul in the right place."

"Why?" He was pretty sure he wouldn't like the answer, but he wanted to hear it from her anyway.

"You're going into battle, Luke. We're both going to need loads of prayer support to get ready. And you're going to need God's grace to pick you up off the ground if you fail."

"Which I won't," he interjected, which only earned him another one of Ruby's looks.

"You say you can't face JetPak without me, but I'm telling you, you shouldn't face that bull without God."

Now she really sounded like Gran. He thought about the open Bible on his kitchen table, feeling more than a little like Ruby, Gran and God had ganged up on him. "You're sure Gran didn't put you up to this?"

"Your grandmother had nothing to do with this. But I expect she'd agree with me that you'd better get your faith back on the right track if you want to do this thing. Consider it part of the treatment plan you think I'm so capable to give you."

Luke sighed. "Well, I always did say you could push me where I didn't want to go."

She sighed, but it wasn't the kind of sigh he used to delight in pulling from her. "You used to go to church all the time, Luke. Why don't you want to go now?"

It'd be easy to give her any one of the half dozen wisecrack answers he gave any of the guys who invited him to cowboy church or the rodeo's Bible study. Still, this was Ruby—she deserved better than that. He sat up and shifted to face her. "At first it was just time. I'd be out so late Saturday night I'd be dead to the world Sunday morning. And I'm working *all* weekend, you know?"

"But lots of rodeo riders are open about their strong faith. Most rodeos I've seen open with prayer."

"And they close with a lot of rowdy partying. I expect you know which one suited me better."

"So you were too hungover to get to church?" He felt her disappointed look in his gut. Gran wasn't the only one who could wield a disparaging glare.

"I told myself that at first. It wasn't the real

reason. It just sort of stopped making sense. I had too many other things calling my name."

Ruby folded her hands in her lap. "Bottles and women, you mean."

He knew it would have to come up at some point. They'd carefully avoided the topic of women up until now. He took a moment to phrase the words right, then answered, "I never loved 'em, Ruby. They were distractions. Amusements. Shallow things that kept me...from thinking about what I'd left behind."

Her face went a bit hard, tight with hurt he knew he'd caused. He had to try and make her understand. He owed her that.

"Truth is, I think I spent the past six years learning the difference between pretty and beautiful. All those women hanging around the rodeo? They sure were pretty." He ducked down into her gaze, needing to see her eyes as he said the rest. "But none of 'em were as beautiful as you. Oh, I liked them well enough, and they made me feel all big and important, but—" *Say it*, he told himself, *say all of it.* "You were the last woman I loved."

She lowered her eyes and went very still. He felt the full depth of how he'd hurt her, his dismissal of the powerful thing that had been between them. He'd tried to tell himself it was just teenage love, two kids who didn't know any better, but he'd never believed it. What they'd had was real, honest, whole-hearted love, the likes of which he'd never felt before or since. He'd lost his chance with her—no, he'd *thrown away* his chance with her—and he'd live with the consequences.

"And I know we can't go back to that," Luke went on when she kept silent, "but I trust you. Deep-down trust, and believe me there isn't much of that where I've been. I need somebody I trust getting me where I need to go now." He waited until she met his eyes. "I need you."

It struck him, right then, that even if she said yes, he wouldn't come out of this completely healed and able to resume his life as if nothing had happened, like he planned. They'd try to keep things concrete and professional for her, but he wouldn't make it. She'd already begun to tug on his heart in a way that wasn't safe for either of them. Maybe that's why he'd been so stupid this week. He'd thought he'd come out of this with an old love remade into a new friend, but that wasn't possible. He was likely to leave his heart in Martins Gap when he left, just like last time.

This ride was going to cost him even more than he thought.

Chapter Sixteen

Mama nudged Ruby's elbow as they sat in church the next week. "Is that who I think it is?"

Ruby nodded. Poor Luke, his arrival at church had been something of a spectacle. He'd probably hoped to slip in without notice, to be just another of the Buckton siblings lining the long pew beside Granny B, but it seemed like everyone went out of their way to note his presence. *I shouldn't enjoy this, Lord*, she confessed, *but I am. Thank for putting that idea in my head at just the right moment.* There were five more Sundays for God to get through to that man before he either rocketed back off to the stars or the bottom fell clean out of his life.

Mama cast her a sideways glance as she

opened her hymnal. "Did you have something to do with that?"

She smiled. "I might have. Let's just say I put a few conditions on our partnership."

The word caught Mama's attention. She put a hand on Ruby's arm. "Be careful, hon. I'd hate to see you hurt again." Mama's slowly earned approval of Luke from years before had gone out the window when he left, and his return hadn't improved her opinion.

"We're friends, Mama."

"Really?" Mama clearly wasn't convinced.

"Well, friends with too much history, maybe, but trust me, I'm not looking to start back up with Luke Buckton. All that was a long while ago, and we're past it."

Mama frowned. "That boy hurt you. Badly."

"And that *man* has apologized. Like I said, we've gotten past it. I have a job to do with him. I told you, Mama, a client like him could do a lot for my practice. I've already gotten several calls for new clients from people who said they'd heard I was treating Luke Buckton." When Mama continued to look skeptical, Ruby added, "Really, I'll be fine."

The start of the hymn ended any further discussion, but Ruby noticed Mama's questioning look when Luke and his niece, Audie, wandered over during the post-service coffee.

"What did you think of the service, Luke?" Ruby tried not to pay attention to how sharp he looked—she'd not seen him dressed up in years, and the turquoise in his lariat tie against the white shirt made his eyes sparkle more than ever.

"Fine enough, I suppose."

Audie leaned in. "That's not what he told me, Miss Ruby."

Ruby couldn't resist. "And what did he tell you?"

"Audie…" Luke warned, his face flushing just a bit.

"Oh, no, Audie, I'd really like to know. He's coming on account of me, after all." That came out with more implications than she would have liked.

"Well," Audie said with great importance in her voice, "he said it wasn't half as boring as he—" the girl's words turned into a squeak as Luke clamped a hand over her mouth.

"As the services I attended on the road," he finished. Ruby had to admire the save, even if it wasn't entirely truthful. His other hand attached itself to his niece's elbow. "Audie, you were showing me where the best cookies are."

"Over there," Ruby offered, not quite hiding her laugh.

"That's not what he said," Audie let slip as Luke led her away.

Mama laughed. "I know Audie's a step-daughter, but I think that girl fits right into the Buckton family, don't you?"

Audie was the daughter of Gunner's wife, Brooke, and as such not Gunner's blood daughter, but Mama was right—she was definitely a Buckton in spirit. From what Ruby had seen around the ranch, Audie and Granny B were two peas in a pod. It amused her to see Luke get taken down a peg or two by someone so young. He laughed it off, but not entirely. She might need to engage Audie's help in keeping Luke on his toes—that girl had the right personality to make a great therapist.

"Hi, Ruby."

Ruby turned, "Rachel, hello." She hadn't noticed the journalist in the service. "Mama, this is Rachel Hartman, the reporter covering Luke's comeback." It still felt odd to put it that way—most of her clients were engaged in healing or treatment. "Comeback" felt a bit too dramatic a term, but Luke had insisted on it.

"It should be quite the event down in San Antonio. Of course, my focus is on how he gets there. His training, his treatment, his hometown life, that sort of thing."

Ruby hid her surprise—San Antonio? That meant being part of the Pro Tour. It made sense; he couldn't really stage an event like that locally, but somehow she'd expected him to do it closer to home and on a slightly smaller scale. Ha—Luke, small scale anything? Still, doing it within the Pro Tour and in San Antonio felt like the launch of his departure to get back to the place where he actually wanted to be—which, of course, it was. "If anyone can do it, it's Luke. He'll have the whole town cheering him on."

"He'll have a lot more than that if I do my job right. People love an underdog story."

Rachel wondered how Luke would take to being labeled an "underdog." He had never fallen second to anyone in anything he did. It was why his injury proved such an emotional setback as well as a physical one. Still, the experience had clearly changed him. The Luke who'd spoken to her with honesty and— dare she say it?—humility at the park, and all week, was a very different man than the boy who'd left years ago. Pastor Theo had preached today on Jacob wrestling the angel and coming away with a limp. That was too much of a coincidence to pin on anyone but

God. *I see You working to get through to him. And now I'm part of it. Watch over both of us, Lord.*

"Will you let me observe some more of your sessions with Luke?" Rachel asked.

"That's up to Luke," Ruby replied. "I'm going to have to push him hard, and he may not want an audience for that."

Rachel offered up a smile. "Oh, I don't know. He strikes me as the kind of man who likes an audience for everything."

"Good for cowboys, not always good for patients," Ruby replied with a shrug. She did think an audience would spur Luke on, but if he hit the end of his patience, it wasn't the kind of thing she wanted the world watching. Was she supposed to be protecting Luke from his appetite for publicity while he trained? Or was that Nolan's job? One thing was certain: this was going to be like no other client she'd ever had. But then, she'd known that from the start.

Rachel leaned in. "Off the record, do you think he can do it?"

Ruby knew enough to see that evading this question would give the wrong impression. Did she have doubts? Of course she did. She expected that even Luke had doubts—not that he'd ever voice them, even to her. "Like I said, if there's anyone who could do it, it's Luke. I wouldn't be on his treatment team if I didn't think he could get back on that bull."

She'd worded her answer carefully. She did believe Luke could get back on the bull. The true question was whether or not he could *stay* there for eight seconds. That, and what damage he'd do in the trying.

Rachel paused, then smiled. She'd clearly recognized the careful balance in Ruby's answer. She tilted her head to one side, then broadened her smile. "Does he know what an asset you are?"

Six years ago, uncertain of her worth, she would have hesitated. She knew, though, how Luke thought of her. He'd been insistent in proclaiming how he needed her for this challenge. She hadn't thought about it until this moment, but she felt appreciated and respected in a more powerful way than just the lovestruck attention Luke had paid her in high school. "Yes," she said with a deep, solid certainty. "I believe he does."

"You know," Rachel replied, "I really do think he'll pull it off." She finished her cup of coffee and turned to Mama, offering a hand. "Nice to meet you, Mrs. Sheldon. You've got a great daughter there."

"Don't I know it," Mama boasted, putting

one arm around Ruby. When Rachel was gone, Mama looked at her. "You didn't know the ride was going to take place in San Antonio, did you?"

Mama always could read her like a book. "No, that's news to me. But I suppose he has to do it somewhere where he can get lots of exposure."

Mama frowned. "Don't you think he should have told you?"

Should he have? Her job was to get him ready. She had no role in the actual ride, except as a spectator. He'd never officially asked her to be there when he did, but she assumed she would be. She wanted to be there. She was too invested not to be there. What did it say that he hadn't shared the San Antonio location with her? "I don't know, Mama, but I'm going to find out."

Luke knew something was up the moment Ruby came around the corner of the church hall. "San Antonio?"

"How'd you hear that?"

Her brows furrowed. "Why does that woman keep telling me things I ought to already know?"

Ouch. He'd promised not to keep things from her. "I just confirmed it last night with

Nolan for the tour stop on September seventeenth. We were going back and forth between there and Houston. I was going to tell you tomorrow, really. I had no idea Nolan would notify Rachel right away."

"Why there instead of closer by?"

"They gave us a better media package. You know I need the biggest bang I can get for this." The package had been even better than he'd dreamed. This comeback was pulling together faster and stronger than even he'd predicted, and it surged through him like a current. *I'm on my way. I won't be down for much longer.*

"Rachel asked to observe another session this week. I told her she needed to ask you."

Luke leaned against the wall. His leg was bothering him this morning, but that was nothing new—he'd been doing twice the number of repetitions Ruby had prescribed. "You could have okayed it."

Ruby crossed her hands over her chest. "I'm going to be working you really hard. You'll fall a lot. Are you sure you want her to see that?"

"Rachel can see me fall, as long as she sees me get back up again." He smiled at her concern. "Besides, falls are dramatic."

"She called you an underdog."

That was a bit of a shocker. He was more accustomed to the term *champion* or *rising star*. Well, if that's what it took to get folks rooting for him, he'd swallow the label. "I can live with that. Besides, I'll only stay an underdog until that ride."

"Then what will you be?"

The question caught him up short... mostly because he didn't have an answer. He wouldn't be a champion—there wasn't enough of the season left to put him back up on top and this was only an exhibition ride. Much as he hated to admit it, Ray was going to take the championship this year, and there wasn't much he could do about it. "Everybody's favorite."

"That's not the same thing as champion." Ruby could follow his thoughts without him ever having to voice them; she knew how he saw the world. He'd miss that back out on the circuit. He'd grown used to her companionship. A bit dependent on it, if he was honest. "You'll be there, won't you? San Antonio? I mean, you have to be. It wouldn't be right if you weren't there."

"We've never talked about it."

"I didn't think we had to. I figured you'd come." He hesitated a moment before adding, "I really want you to come."

She smiled. "I'll be there. Someone has to keep an eye on you while you go crazy celebrating your victory."

"That's Nolan's job." He reached for Ruby's hand. "I don't want you there as my babysitter. I want you there as my friend." As he ran his thumb along the back of her hand the way he always had those years ago, he realized he didn't mean it. He wanted her there as something more than just a friend. "Come to San Antonio. See what this whole crazy thing is like."

After the way he'd told her all those years ago that she couldn't come with him, couldn't be part of his life anymore once he went on the circuit, that was a loaded request, and he knew it. He'd left her behind, half to please his new agent and half out of the knowledge that Ruby wasn't cut out for that lifestyle. And she wasn't—back then.

She was different now. He was, too. The hard partying rang dull and tinny in his ears now. More than a wild night, he craved someone he could trust. Someone who believed in him for more than just his earning power or fan base or how much the camera liked him.

For him, now, she'd be the perfect companion on the circuit.

With one glaring exception: she'd never go.

To pick up where they left off—where they truly left off, not just this pretense of a friendship they'd strung between them, she'd either need to leave Martins Gap or he'd need to stay. Both were impossible, and they knew it.

Still, as he stood there with her hand in his the way it used to be between them, Luke found himself wanting that relationship back. He caught the spark of his touch in her eyes, saw the "what if" he'd begun to think himself.

"Come to San Antonio," he repeated. "It's beautiful there. We'll do it up right. I'll show you how it can be."

He took her other hand, so that he now held both.

"I'll think about it," she said, her voice a bit breathy.

He gave her a smoldering smile. He still knew exactly how to sweep her off her feet. "You do that." Not everything had changed— he could convince her to say yes, he could flood her with charm until she couldn't think straight.

At least that's what the old Luke would have done. He surprised himself by not wanting to pull that kind of stunt anymore. Who was this man who now wouldn't stoop to anything to get what he wanted?

The answer came to him like a tap on the shoulder. The underdog. A man who's been down knows the value of true friends, of real loyalty. The line about the difference between "pretty" and "beautiful" had been no line. His suffering had helped him look past the superficial and understand what really mattered. In these past weeks Luke had come to see that the very things that made Ruby seem like a bad fit for the circuit back then made her the companion he needed now.

San Antonio may be all they got together. They'd return to their separate lives after that, though he believed they'd always stay in touch from now on. As she squeezed his hands and headed back to her mom, San Antonio burned in his chest for more than just his chance to master JetPak. San Antonio would be his chance to give Ruby the farewell she deserved. Because he knew, now, that a truc goodbye is not the same thing as being left behind.

The woman Ruby was now was no woman to be left behind. Which made it all the harder to know she was a woman he couldn't keep by his side.

Chapter Seventeen

The remaining weeks flew past at lightning speed. Luke behaved in his therapy sessions, worked harder than Ruby had ever seen him work and pressed forward with such determination that she began to believe he truly would pull his exhibition off. He showed up at church every Sunday, often joining her and Oscar for their Sunday afternoon romps in the park. They would talk, and laugh and pretend neither of them felt the constant pull toward what they had once been to each other.

As the fateful weekend in September arrived, Ruby found herself driving into San Antonio with a mixture of dread and excitement. They'd worked so hard to get here. He'd pursued his training with a single-minded zeal, relaxing only when she commanded him to do so. So now, the crucial moments were upon them.

Them, not just him, because Ruby no longer fooled herself that her life wouldn't be forever changed by what happened here Saturday night. He would either succeed and depart from her life, or he would fail and then who knew what would happen next?

Ruby had seen rodeo events before, but this one felt ten times larger in every respect. Yes, the touring division wasn't on the same scale as the world championships—those big-purse divisions had their events in places like New York City and Las Vegas—but this event was still big, loud, frantic and relentless. The arena could have held all of Martins Gap five times over, and the thing went on for days.

Luke told her the whole event had a prize purse topping one million dollars, and it looked like it. Carnivals, shows and contests filled the grounds and packed every surrounding hotel for miles around. Concerts with big stars gave a Hollywood glitz to the place that Ruby could see suited Luke's love for the "larger than life."

Luke's ride of JetPak had been tacked on to the bull riding night as an exhibition ride—no competition but loads of visibility. As such, Luke wasn't competing against anyone but the bull and himself. Ruby couldn't decide if that was a good thing or a bad one.

Her hotel room had been paid for by the jeans company sponsoring Luke's "Comeback vs. JetPak"—as it had been billed. He'd been shuttled from interview to interview over the last few days, necessitating that she scoot in to supervise his ongoing exercises during gaps in his schedule. They'd finally managed to get a pair of free hours on Friday night, during which Luke insisted they head to the carnival rather than squeeze in more therapy. She was grateful he'd chosen to relax a bit, as he'd been tightly wound since arriving in the city.

"What do you think?" Luke said as they bit into a pair of deep-fried Oreos.

The fried cookies were absurdly delicious. "I could probably only get away with eating one of these every five years. Is there anything they don't fry here? How does anyone survive eating this stuff all the time?" Ruby replied, licking her lips.

"Hard to say. Nolan is a fan of the chicken-fried bacon, but then again Nolan sees a cardiologist."

Seeing Luke in his element like this, it was easy to see that Nolan wasn't the influence she'd assumed. Nolan simply cleared the path for the crazy pace Luke set for himself. A frenzy which seemed to feed Luke as much as it made her dizzy. Looking at his schedule and the way he sailed through it with aplomb, she would never guess the man had been seriously injured. It made her that much more grateful for this small break for him to wind down a little.

As they finished off another fried confection—and Ruby began to wonder if the jeans she'd brought would still fit on the drive home—Luke pointed to the event's enormous Ferris wheel. "Wanna?" he asked, his eyes lit up in invitation.

Ruby looked up. "It's huge."

Luke nodded, adjusting his hat as he followed her gaze up to the top. "Best view of the place. I expect you can see the River Walk from up there. And, darlin', this is the calmest ride I'll consent to go on, so now's your chance. Skip this and I might drag you onto that." He pointed toward something doing crazy corkscrews in the night sky that made Ruby's stomach drop out just watching it.

It would get Luke sitting down for at least twenty minutes—something she hadn't seen him do all day. "Sure."

Suddenly, she felt eighteen again, waiting in line at the local carnival as colored lights flashed around them. When Luke took her hand to help her up into the Ferris wheel car, she let him. When he didn't let go but squeezed it tight as the car ascended the great glistening arc, she told herself it was okay to cling to him—it was a mildly unnerving thing to be up so high amid so many people, after all.

"Look at it, Ruby, all spread out and sparkling." She supposed that paradise to him would look very much like this place—full of lights and sounds and thrills. Ruby's idea of perfection would look very different—calmer and less frantic, full of people she knew and loved rather than a bunch of strangers.

It was just another way they were different.

The Ferris wheel slowly moved toward the top as each car filled. Luke pointed up to the star-filled sky. "See?" he said, gesturing wide with his hand as if the place was his personal kingdom. "Best view of the place, just like I said."

She felt a rush at the splendor of the view. "It is amazing." A breeze whirled around them, and she didn't mind when he put his arm around her to shield her from the chill. It felt so much like old times, back before everything grew painful and complicated. She couldn't deny it was fun, thrilling even, to see

Luke in his element. "I didn't think I would like it much," she admitted, "but it's fun."

"A far cry from Martins Gap, that's for sure."

Ruby pointed to one of the smaller venues. "You could fit the whole town just in there. Your niece is going to love the sheep and the goats when she gets here." All the Bucktons were scheduled to arrive tomorrow in advance of Luke's big ride on JetPak. "I'm glad they'll all be here for you."

He settled back against the cab, stretching out his bad leg the way he always did when it bothered him. "Me, too, but I'm glad to have some time before they show up." He looked at her. "Time with you." He let his head fall back, taking in the stars. "I can unwind with you, you know? You're probably the only person in this whole place who doesn't want something from me."

So it did tax him. He made like it was all great fun, but she suspected the constant attention and endless demands were more draining than he admitted. "How are you feeling?" Today was the last day she could work him hard—and she had—so she suspected his leg hurt a bit. Otherwise, from a physical standpoint, Luke was as ready as he'd ever be.

"Fine. Mighty fine." He drew the words out with a drawl. The car began its descent around the wheel, picking up a bit of speed. "We must be full up. Here we go."

The ride became a series of stomach-lurching swoops down and up, pulling whoops from Luke and squeals from Ruby. Luke threw his hands up in the air while Ruby clutched on the bar that stretched across their laps. The pure, silly fun rejuvenated her from all the pressures of the past few days, from the worries over how bad Grandpa had looked when she left and the concerned looks Mama had been giving her for days. One little nostalgic slice of happiness in a place where everything seemed too huge and too important. Ruby laughed and screamed, hiding her eyes one moment and popping them wide open the next.

Then—because there was always a "then"—the wheel slowed to begin letting riders off. She caught her breath as the cab began to work its way up the wheel. So much of her wanted the ride to last longer, to spend a few more minutes being silly and effortless with Luke. Over the past weeks they'd managed to capture the best part of what they'd had together back then, but at the same time it was different, older, truer—if that was a word—because of who they were now.

Luke couldn't remember a time he'd laughed this hard. He smiled all the time since he'd arrived here in San Antonio—both because he wanted to and because he had to. But laugh? Real throw-your-head-back and laugh? He hadn't done that in ages. Ruby's squeals seem to tickle all the way down his back, and he felt lit up like the banks of lights below them.

It didn't take any effort. Being with Ruby had always been effortless. He'd spent so much time trying to impress the right people and say the right things and make the right connections out on the tour that he'd forgotten what it felt like just to "be" with someone. No agenda, no conversation to make happen, no impression to be made, just *be*.

When the car stilled at the top of the wheel, with the whole wide sky of stars sparkling above them and in Ruby's brown eyes, it was as if his heart refused to stay put. He turned Ruby to face him, delighting at all the joy he saw in her face. "Let me kiss you, Ruby. Just once, here, now, or I think I'll die of wanting to."

He wasn't the kind of man who asked for

a kiss. He knew just how take one from her if he wanted to. And he knew he could take one now, and the consequences wouldn't be too dire. He could overwhelm her with charm until she gave in. After all, his specialty in life had always been knowing how to get exactly what he wanted. But right now, what he wanted most of all was for her to willingly choose to give this to him.

She nodded, not even realizing her tongue licked those impossibly pink lips in a way that drove him crazy. He would have thrown a thousand dollars he didn't have down to the man at the controls if it would stop the wheel for an hour and strand him up here with Ruby.

Luke slipped one hand around the back of her neck, the soft waves of her hair brushing the back of his palm. She smelled so good—soft and delicate but still bright and spirited. When he settled his mouth over hers, it all came rushing back. All the star-struck love, the way she made him feel as if he could own the world, the way his heart felt as if it found the one place on Earth it truly fit. Martins Gap was where he was born, but Ruby had always been his true home.

But this time, it wasn't a boy kissing a girl, it was a man kissing a woman—and the difference shook him. Ruby was warm and strong and *equal*. He hadn't expected that to course through him the way it did, but her strength lit something in him he'd long forgotten was even there. He'd spent the past years being liked, admired, wanted, pushed, pulled and even judged, but kissing Ruby reminded Luke what it was like to be *loved*. When her arms slipped around his neck, a hole opened up inside him. One he'd kept covered for years, one he'd convinced himself didn't even exist anymore.

Who was he kidding? He couldn't be friends with this woman. He couldn't hope to be anything but in love with her. He fell right back in love with her with every kiss. Back when he was eighteen, he'd have told the world he couldn't love Ruby Sheldon more than he did. Right now told him how wrong he was. What he felt now as a man was truer, deeper, stronger than what that boy had felt.

By the time they were halfway to the bottom of the ride, Ruby pulled away, breathing hard. "Luke…" Her eyes were wide, and he could feel her heart slam against his chest to match his own wild heartbeat.

"I know," he said, breathless himself. "I know."

She tried to pull away from him a bit, but he wouldn't let her. He wasn't about to back away from this moment or let her do the same. She ran one hand through her hair, flustered. He understood the response—he felt mixed up inside, too. Only it was a right kind of mixed up, a worth-it kind of jumbled that felt like things falling messily into place. A perfect order he couldn't quite see yet but could believe was possible.

"This isn't right," she said.

"Are you sure?" he questioned. "It's complicated—I get that—but it feels right to me. We were good together then, maybe we'll be better together now." Their car was only a few stops away from the bottom and Luke fought the panic that told him if he let Ruby back away now, he'd lose her. *I can't lose her. Not now when I've just figured out how much I need her.*

Ruby flung her hand at the lights and noise drawing closer. "This is you. This isn't me."

Luke lay his hand against her cheek. "No, darlin'. *This* is me." He looked right into her eyes, deep into the velvety brown of them—a color he'd never ever forgotten. "This is us. The rest is just window dressing. We can find a way."

"We can't find what isn't there, Luke. What I feel doesn't change facts."

There was so much struggle in her tone.

"What do you feel?" He felt sure the current that surged through him right now was as strong for her. He'd felt it in her kiss, but he needed to hear it in her words.

"Too much."

He had to smile at that. "Ain't that the truth."

The car moved again—two more stops and the ride would be over. "It can't work," she said. "I still care for you but I can't see how it would work."

Luke still loved Ruby. He knew it with a certainty that dared any of the facts to stand in his way. "Do we have to see how right now? Can we just take today, and tomorrow, and work it from there?"

"If I say yes to this…"

She didn't finish the sentence, but he knew her well enough to know what she was thinking. It'd have to be forever. Did he have forever in him? Did he even know what forever looked like? Ruby would need promises, assurances, vows, and those things were foreign territory to him. Luke went with the only truth he knew for sure. "I want to try, Ruby. I want to try so bad I can barely breathe. Don't back away. Not now, not yet. Give us a chance." The cab started descending again and he kissed her with everything he had to give. "Give us a chance," he repeated.

She'd always told him she loved him with her eyes more than anything else, and he could see the love now. It shone, true but fragile, despite the flashing lights and sounds of the carnival now surrounding them. Luke held on to her hand, an unspoken "I won't let you go." His heart glowed in gratitude when she kept her hand in his as they got off the ride. Holding her hand felt like a lifeline right now—one he desperately needed. "Let's get out of this noise, okay?"

"I'd like that. But where?"

His heart knew the place before his brain did. It was the last place he usually wanted to be before a ride, but somehow it felt like the only place he'd find any peace right now. "I know where. Come on."

Chapter Eighteen

The security guard gave Luke a suspicious glare when Luke showed his badge. Ruby suspected he had any number of reasons to question why Luke would want to be in the arena the night before a ride. The concert had let out, and the stage crews were working on the dirt floor that would host tomorrow's rodeo events. Even with all that noise, the place still held a looming emptiness, a canyon of vacant seats.

He led her to one of the rows overlooking the stock pens. In hours it would be filled with the snuffling and shuffling of bulls and horses, but for now it was a vastly vacant space. The dark emptiness made it feel close and huge at the same time. He sat down, pulling her down next to him by the hand he'd continued to hold since the Ferris wheel. He clung to her. He'd never done that before.

"Give me tonight and tomorrow, Ruby. Just these two days. We'll figure it out after that, I know we will." His hand still held tight to hers.

She wanted to feel as certain as Luke seemed to, but it eluded her. There were too many complications in the way. She couldn't plunge headlong into a wall of obstacles the way Luke could, and all she could see—when Luke wasn't blinding her senses with irresistible kisses—were obstacles. Dozens of them.

Luke grew quiet, and she looked up to see his eyes on the row of chutes below them. One of those would pull open tomorrow to unleash his battle against JetPak. What would it feel like to have your whole future hinge on eight seconds? To have everything boil down to one moment like that?

"I'm scared." He said it softly, quickly, as if he could barely stand to voice the words.

She felt her heart crack open just then. As if her heart needed to see him drop his guard before it would admit to the power of what still flowed between them.

She wrapped both her hands around his. Whatever would come—or not come—between them, she knew what that admission cost him. "You're ready," she said. "You know you are."

"My body's ready."

She looked at him, puzzled.

"I'm not so sure my soul is."

Oh, Father, he's looking for You. He's ready to come back to You. "God doesn't care what happens tomorrow."

Luke practically snorted, making her realize she hadn't put that quite right. She burst into laughter as he said, "Well, that's not very comforting. I kinda hoped I had the Almighty on my side."

"I said that wrong. He cares what you want. He knows how much this means to you. What I meant to say was that His love for you and your value to Him won't change no matter what happens tomorrow. You can trust Him with the outcome. *I'm* trusting Him with the outcome." *The outcome of a lot of things.*

"I know that. I knew it before, though I'd sort of forgotten it for a while." He cracked a smile. "But some pushy therapist made me promise to plant my backside in a church pew a while back, and I guess some of it stuck. Or re-stuck."

The comfort of hearing that spread a warm glow in her chest. She didn't want to have to watch God break Luke to get his attention.

"I'm really glad to hear that. It makes tomorrow easier for me—and for you."

Luke slumped down in his seat, running one hand through his hair. "Oh, nothing about tomorrow is gonna be easy." His eyes wandered to the chute gates again, and she could feel the tension radiate out into the air around him. He lifted his gaze to take in the huge arena. "But as tough as it is, I've missed this. The lights, the sound, the crowd, the all-or-nothing of it. Life feels two hundred percent in here, always did. Tough, hard, but the highs were as high as the lows were low, you know?"

She didn't. She could appreciate the spectacle, but to live in a world like this? Do this week after week? Sure, not all events were on this scale, but that wouldn't alter how foreign the world felt. The "all-or-nothing" that he loved had no appeal at all to her. How could she feel so much for the man and so little for his world? "You've always belonged here."

He must have caught the resignation in her voice, for he turned to her. "I belong with you. It took me all this time to figure it out again. How we make this work is just another problem we'll solve, like we've solved all the other stuff." He ran one hand through her hair, sending tingles down her neck. "I want to get on the bull tomorrow knowing you're here waiting for me afterward. I'm not asking for more than tomorrow right now."

He left a small, soft kiss on her cheek. The tenderness of that undid her more than the power of his earlier kisses. It made her mind spiral into all kinds of "what if" fantasies about who they could be now. She knew those to be dreams, but didn't dreams sometimes come true?

Just as many times, they didn't. Tomorrow would tell.

She put her hand on top of Luke's "I think it's time we both got some rest, don't you?"

"There you go, always looking out for me." He rose, slowly and carefully unfolding his long legs from the tight stadium seating, and extended a hand to pull her up. "I'll sleep better, having kissed you. Am I allowed to say that?"

She laughed as she rose. "It's cheesy, but I'll allow it."

He slipped an arm around her waist once they were standing. "Pray for me tonight, will you?"

The glow in her chest doubled. "I will, just as I have been all along, but I think you ought to do some praying for yourself. And not just the part in the arena at the start of the event."

"Believe it or not, I was planning to before you even said something. You're good for me, Ruby. Always were. I want to show you how good I can be for you. To you. I know I've got a lot of time and things to make up for."

All that felt far distant in the past. She was surprised by that, thinking the old wound would sting forever. When she'd gotten out of that car on the Blue Thorn Ranch all those weeks ago, she was only expecting closure. Maybe even a little justice, and if she was brutally honest, some payback. She'd gotten so much more. She'd healed right alongside him. That had to count for something, didn't it? "We are good for each other. But…"

He put one finger to her lips. "No 'but's. Not yet. I know they're there, but let's just leave those for later. You're always saying God's a big God, maybe now's the time we learn how to trust Him with the answers we can't see yet. I'm not asking for forever Ruby—I don't have the right to that yet. I'm only asking for tomorrow."

She could give him that. She wanted to give him that. Ruby simply nodded, the moment feeling too big for words.

His smile could have lit the arena. "I'll take you on back to your hotel now. Thanks for a wonderful night. Best I've had in forever."

A large part of her wanted to say the same, but she simply kept quiet as they walked hand in hand out of the arena and back toward the hotel.

5:45 a.m.

Ruby stared at the yellow numbers of the complicated hotel room clock and the soft glow they gave to the unfamiliar room. She hoped Luke had gotten a better rest than she had, for she'd tossed and turned most of the night. Her mind had been whirring in too many directions to make much sleep possible, and she reached for the light switch with an unwelcome weariness. Today felt too big to handle on so little sleep.

Luke's ride was set for around four, just after the opening of the special finale championship showcase event. While Luke's day would be jam-packed, hers was surprisingly empty until the event. *I'd better catch a nap this afternoon if I can*, she thought to herself as she yawned. If he met with victory, Luke would want to celebrate all night. Right now, Ruby felt like she'd barely make it to Audie's bedtime, much less Luke's.

She padded over to the window and pulled open the curtains to see the beginnings of a sunrise peep up over the event grounds.

Now that it was quiet and layered in pastels, the place seemed to suit her better than its loud and flashing state last night. Maybe all the rodeo world wasn't so garish as she thought. Perhaps outside the actual events, a different world—a different life—could be had. Maybe Luke was right and there was a way to mesh their futures. She'd heard most rodeo cowboys worked on Sundays, so they had cowboy church at times they could attend and places convenient to their life. It could be done. There were grounded, faithful family men who also worked the rodeo circuit.

But that wasn't Luke. At least not yet. *You'll have to help me on this one, Lord*, she prayed. *I can't see my way through clearly at all.*

First things first. Ruby followed the directions on the tiny hotel coffeepot and set it to brew while she climbed into the shower. The bathroom here was twice the size of the one at home, shiny and luxurious. The kingsize bed felt huge and indulgent—a waste of a sleepless night, to be sure. A deliciously long, hot shower would do her a world of good. There were certainly lots of things to like in this life, even though she knew most bull riders were barely scraping by financially. Would Luke have to go back to that scrabble of a life, or would he relaunch near the top and just keep going?

Indulging in the soft, fluffy bathrobe that came with her hotel room, Ruby sat down on the bed with her coffee and checked her phone.

She nearly dropped the coffee when she saw three messages and a "Call me now" text from Mama.

Shaking, it took her a minute to remember how to listen to her voicemail messages. When she finally got it to work, a trio of panicked calls met her ears. Call one was "I'm calling an ambulance for Grandpa. He doesn't know where he is or who I am." Call two was "We're in the ER now, and he's angry. He's fighting the doctors. I've never seen him like this. Where are you, Ruby?"

Call three was from five minutes ago—she must have had the hair dryer going—and the worst of all. "Why haven't you answered? They're admitting Pop and saying things I don't understand. They're talking about him having to have a breathing tube. I need you, Ruby. Call me!"

Grandpa. He'd been feeling badly all week, given to coughing fits and such, but she'd talked herself out of the idea of his being in any danger because she wanted to be here.

A twist of guilt gripped her stomach alongside the fear. Grandpa was frail. He could die and she wouldn't be there. Mama feared this most of all—losing Grandpa faster than she could bear to say goodbye—and Ruby was hours away.

It didn't take a moment's thought. Ruby threw on the nearest set of clothes and began stuffing everything else into the little suitcase she'd brought. Three hours was a long drive, but every second she stayed here was another chance for Grandpa to slip away. She called her mother as she zipped up the bag.

"Ruby! Where have you been, child? I was sure I'd wake you up when I called a minute ago, not find you gone—away from your phone." Mama's voice was sharp with fear and tears.

"I woke up early. I was in the shower. I'm on my way Mama. I'll be there in three hours. Are you at Memorial?" She prayed they hadn't found a need to move Grandpa into Austin for more extensive treatment, even though it was closer to San Antonio than Martins Gap.

"Yes. They got an IV and fluids into him, but they're still considering putting him on a breathing machine. It's like he just woke up a different man at four a.m.—he was so confused and upset with these horrible coughing fits. They could barely get him into the ambulance."

Ruby yanked on her shoes. "What have they told you?"

"Some kind of infection. Kidney maybe, liver maybe, but they also think he has pneumonia. He's got such a high fever. They're putting so many antibiotics into him I can't keep them straight. They're going to do a chest X-ray in about a half hour. He wasn't like this when he went to bed last night—it all happened so fast." Mama's voice broke. "I don't want them to put a tube down Pop's throat. I'm not ready to say goodbye to him. Not yet."

Ruby scanned the room for any remaining belongings, letting one sharp stab of the day she'd leave behind push through the certain knowledge that right now, Martins Gap was where she needed to be. A rodeo comeback was a fine thing, but Mama's fear and Grandpa's health were much more important.

I should call him, she thought to herself as she pushed the elevator buttons. *Stop by his room*. But what would she say? He had his family with him today, she needed to be with hers. He'd be upset, but he'd understand if she used the right words. If he truly cared for her the way he seemed to last night, he'd know she needed to leave.

But it would throw him. On a day he couldn't afford to be thrown—literally. A quick check of her phone told her it wasn't even 7:00 a.m. *I'll think about what to say on the road, then call him in an hour or so.*

Checking out took far too long. Finding her car in the vast parking lot took too long, everything took too long. She wanted to wish herself back to Martins Gap in a heartbeat, be able to reach for her mother's hand instead of looking for the highway onramp she missed the first time.

Don't take him now, she pleaded to God as she pulled out onto the wide highway, empty at the early hour. *Not yet. If You are calling him home, please wait until I get there. I'm trusting Grandpa and Luke to your care, Lord. Don't give me reason to regret being far from either of them.*

Forty minutes later, while she refilled the gas tank, Ruby stared at her cell phone. The words to tell Luke she wouldn't be there for his ride simply hadn't come. Fatigue and fear kept all the right things to say just out of reach. *I'll call him from the hospital when I know more. He won't miss me until after the ride anyway, maybe it's kinder not to tell him yet. Or I can always have Granny B tell him. She'll know what to say and how to say it.*

Ruby would be with him in spirit, and in prayer. She might even get Ellie or Gunner to send her cell phone video of the ride while it happened. She'd find a way to be both places at once the best she could.

Going home to be with Mama and Grandpa is the right thing, isn't it, Lord? Ruby prayed as she paid for her gas and a large strong coffee to keep her going. *It's not a perfect solution, but I don't know what else to do.*

Chapter Nineteen

Luke gaped at the desk clerk. "She can't have checked out. Look again."

"I'm sorry, sir, but Miss Sheldon checked out before I got on shift at seven this morning. All I've got is the record here, and that's what it says."

"Did she say why?"

The clerk gave him the look such a question deserved—of course the guy wouldn't know why Ruby had left. But *he* ought to know—he had to know. He'd told her he wouldn't have time to see her before the ride, so she wasn't expecting him, but he hadn't slept well and wanted to see her. Needed to see her, to get back the grounding he had to feel for this afternoon.

He needed Ruby and she was gone. Luke turned in a slow circle, one hand scraping across his chin, at a complete loss for what to do. It was after ten. He had a final interview with Rachel Hartman in an hour. His family would be here an hour after that. How was he going to find Ruby in this huge place in under an hour? If she was still here at all.

Instead of being helpful, his family's impending arrival just made him feel worse. He'd planned to tell Gran before the ride how he was going to try and make a go of it with Ruby. He'd arranged for Ruby to sit with his family. He wanted to look up into the stands just before he settled onto that bull and know they were there for him. How could he do that now?

Luke stepped away from the front desk to stare at his cell phone again. He had to have somehow missed a call or text from her, right? Nothing. He started to call her, then stopped, stunned by a thought. *Did I scare her away?* He'd come on awfully strong last night. It wouldn't be the first time he pushed too hard for something he wanted so badly. And he did want her. He needed her by his side. Once he'd figured that out, it was as if he couldn't stop himself from convincing her that's where she belonged.

He sank down into a lobby chair, his head in his hands. He'd had a terrible night's sleep, and now this. For a guy who needed to be at the top of his game, he felt lost and worried.

I didn't push too hard, did I, Lord? Tell me I didn't scare her away. You want me coming to You, well now You've got it. Only if You know me as well as Ruby says You do, You know I can't pull this off without her. So here I am. Find her. Bring her back to me.

Fatigue, worry and even anger boiled up in equal parts as he pushed the elevator button for his hotel room floor. His plan had been to surprise her by taking her to breakfast, but he might as well just get room service now. He didn't want to be with anyone if he couldn't be with Ruby.

Luke grabbed an apple from the fruit basket Nolan had sent while he paced around the room waiting for his breakfast. How could Ruby leave? Why would she leave? It had to be something huge—an emergency with her mom or grandfather or something—but why wouldn't she have found a way to let him know if that was the case? It wasn't like Ruby to just leave.

But it was like him. The realization soured the apple in his mouth. Hadn't he done the same thing? Just leave? Oh, he'd told her why he was leaving—and had been cruel about it besides. Some part of him had wanted to make her hate him back then, to frame it as a dramatic breakup rather than just the cowardly discarding it truly was. Nolan had fed him a bunch of hogwash about how he needed to be "handsome and available," how a wild lifestyle was an asset to a bull rider trying to make a name for himself, how a sweet hometown girl wouldn't fit the image he'd need to portray.

Nolan had been wrong. Luke tossed the apple into the garbage. Tomorrow, he'd sit down with Nolan and hammer out a way to make his career work on the terms he wanted. Terms that included Ruby.

He picked up his cell phone and texted four words to Ruby: Please PLEASE call me.

His thumbs hovered over the keyboard, itching to add three other words. *I love you.* He did love her. Hadn't ever stopped loving her, now that he thought about it. Only a text message wasn't the way to say those words, not for the first time in six years. He'd tell her the minute he saw her—if he could figure out how to make that happen.

Luke stared at the phone, willing it to light up with a reply. It didn't. Part of him yearned to hunt her down, to find her and tell her how he felt right now, to make sure something awful hadn't happened and that he'd only spooked her with his over-the-top display last night. It wasn't possible that she'd really left him for good. He'd reached out, now he had to wait.

He hated waiting for anything, much less this.

What's the point in making her unreachable, Lord? Could it be that the best thing he could do right now was give her time? On a day like today, it felt impossible. He needed her. He'd never been more aware of how much he needed her.

And really, how selfish was that? He'd done this whole thing on his terms. He'd never really asked her if she wanted to come—just told her to be here. He'd made the hotel reservations for her before he'd bothered to ask. Had he pressured her into coming somewhere she'd rather not be because it's what he wanted? He'd turned on every ounce of his persuasive charm last night, determined to win her over. To make her do *what he wanted.*

A man who really cared for her would have thought about what *she* wanted. It stung that his first thought upon finding her gone wasn't concern for her welfare or worry, it was panic that he didn't have what he needed. *I'm ashamed of that, Lord. I don't want to be that man. I want to be whoever it is that Ruby needs me to be. Only I don't know what that is or how to make it happen.* Maybe that was the faith and transformation Ruby was always talking about. He'd started to feel some of it during his weeks at church, when Pastor Theo talked about men who let themselves be changed by their faith so that they could do the extraordinary tasks God set in front of them.

I've got a whopper of a task in front of me today. I'm gonna be changed by it, either way. I don't know if I've got it in me to trust You without Ruby here to back me up. Some big, clear help right about now would go a long way.

Luke made himself sit still. Made himself wait and listen for whatever was going to show itself. But there was nothing. No great revelation, no call or text from Ruby, no holy peace or strength or whatever it was men of God were supposed to feel. Just plain old Luke up against a bull.

Only now it was plain, tired, worried, stressed Luke up against the ride of a lifetime. Talk about odds to make a man shake in his boots. He rubbed his leg, the flare of pain that always came with stress reminding him how his body couldn't be entirely trusted just yet.

Luke jumped when his cell phone buzzed in his hands, but it was only the alarm function reminding him he had an interview with Rachel in ten minutes. Once all this started, it would be like a flash flood picking up speed and force until it dropped him, ready or not, on top of JetPak.

Grandpa looked bad. Like a shadow of himself, pale and thin against the impersonal white sheets of the hospital bed. He looked too much like a dying man, as if the life were draining out of him right in front of her eyes. Ruby could see why Mama had spent the last hours in near constant tears—she felt her own throat continually thick with emotion since walking in the hospital doors.

"Are you Laura's daughter?" Ruby turned at the question to see the kind face of a doctor behind her.

"Yes." Mama had gone for coffee, having been up most of the night, so Ruby took the opportunity to ask the question she most dreaded of the internist. "How is he, really?"

"It's touch and go, I admit, but he looks like a fighter."

He was, Ruby thought. *I'm not so sure anymore.* She wiped away a tear. "I'll be so sorry to lose him."

The doctor, a middle-aged woman with the kindest eyes, put a hand on her shoulder. "He might pull through. We're doing everything we can to speed his healing. Try to keep up hope. And keep encouraging him. Patients can hear even when they seem unresponsive, and it will help him fight."

The doctor pulled the stethoscope from her neck and began doing various checkups on Grandpa. Ruby sank into the creaky vinyl chair, the world spinning chaotically around her. She checked her watch. 11:30 a.m. Luke's family should be in San Antonio by now.

Please PLEASE call me. She'd seen the text, so she knew he was aware she wasn't in San Antonio. Was he angry? Concerned? Anxious? She owed him a response. In truth, she wanted to hear his voice, as much as she hoped he wanted to hear hers. The timing of all this seemed so cruel.

Mama came back in the room just as the doctor was finishing. "Is everything all right?" she nearly gasped.

"Just a routine check, Mrs. Sheldon," the doctor said in calm tones. "There's been no change. Did you get something to eat?"

Mama set her paper cup of coffee down. "I'm not hungry."

The doctor shot Ruby a look. "The best

thing you can do for Grandpa right now," Ruby said as she hauled herself off the chair, "is take care of yourself as well. I need to make a phone call. I'll go grab us some lunch and bring it back."

"Good idea," said the doctor. "Wise daughter you raised there."

"Phone call?" Mama said, one eyebrow cautiously raised.

"Luke. I didn't talk to him before I left." Ruby felt it best not to get any more into that with Mama right now.

Ducking out of the hospital room, Ruby found a quiet, sunny corner. *Give me the words*, she prayed, before dialing Luke's phone number.

He picked up immediately. "Ruby," Luke's voice was filled with relief. She could hear him turn his voice away. "Hey, look guys, I gotta take this. Give me ten minutes, okay?" There was a lot of noise behind him on the line as he came back to her. "Where are you? What's going on?"

The sound of his voice brought the tears right back to the surface. She should have told him right away. Why did she make this so complicated when people hurting should be the simplest thing in the world? "It's Grandpa. Luke, I don't think he's gonna make it."

"Ruby. Oh, mercy, Ruby, why didn't you come get me? I went crazy when I found out you'd left."

"I told myself I shouldn't. It's your big day and all."

"I was crazy, Ruby, because I thought I'd driven you away. Look, I need you, I want you here—I won't lie that I miss you like crazy right now—but I would have told you to go. Helped you to go."

Had he changed that much? Had she let her history with him, the way he'd left her back then, cloud what they could have been to each other today? Ruby leaned back against the wall, unable to find words for the tumble of thoughts in her head.

Luke clearly caught on to the hesitation, for his next words were soft and choked with emotion. "Look, I know you have reasons to doubt me. I left you high and dry all those years ago for all the wrong reasons. So you had every right to think I'd be selfish about today. But I'm not that man anymore. I don't know how to prove it to you, but I'll find a way. I need you today, and you need me. And I hate every mile between us right now."

That's exactly how she felt. She loathed the distance between them because right now she craved his arms around her and she knew he craved the same. She'd spent so much time bearing witness to other people's pain, and now she needed someone beside her in her own. She knew now, deep down, that the person she wanted was Luke. "I don't know how we do this. Today, the rest of it, any of it."

He exhaled. "Me neither. If God has a plan in all this, He hasn't shared it with me yet."

She could almost manage a damp laugh. "You asked?"

"I begged."

Those two words were a comfort to her heart. "I want to be there for you."

"I want to be there for you."

There was their relationship—in all its power and all its problems—right there in that exchange. They wanted to be there for each other, but the whole world was in the way.

"Ruby?"

"Yes?"

"I love you. I hate that I'm saying it on the phone instead of staring into your eyes, but I figure now's a good time to lay that on the table."

She lost her battle to the tears. "Oh, Luke."

"Is that a good 'Oh, Luke,' or a bad 'Oh, Luke'? And before you answer, keep in mind

I'm about to risk my future on a huge angry animal in front of thousands of people."

She laughed. Oh, how she needed the fearlessness he could bring to her life. "You already know which, you crazy cowboy."

"I could use a little affirmation today."

"Yes, I love you. I don't think I ever really stopped."

She could almost hear his smile over the phone. "Yeah, I know." His tone glowed. "Close your eyes and think about me holding you for a moment, will you?"

She did. For an instant, the miles between them evaporated.

"Feel that?" he said. "Can you feel it?"

Ruby wiped the stream of tears sliding down her cheeks. "Yeah, I can."

"That's how we do this."

She grabbed a tissue from her pocket. "How are you? I mean, are you ready for the ride?"

"I'll get there." She recognized all he didn't say in that response.

A thought popped into her head. "Look around you. Is there anything red?"

"Huh?"

"Humor me," Ruby said, feeling a tiny sliver of strength return. "Is there anything red?"

"Um…" There was a pause on the line. "One of the guys has a bandana."

"Get it."

"What?"

"Get the bandana."

After a moment, she heard Luke say, "Hey, Craig, would it be okay if I borrowed that for today? Crazy reason."

"Well, okay," came a voice from across the room.

Luke returned. "I've got it. What am I supposed to do with it?"

"Hold it. It's from me. It's me there with you. Put it someplace where I can see it when you ride. I'll find a way to watch from here."

"You're crazy, you know that? That's the wrong color bandana for a Buckton—Blue Thorn Ranch always has a boatload of blue bandanas."

"But it's the right one from me."

His laugh was soft and intimate. "I think I just fell for you a little bit more."

"Take care, Luke. Ride well, and I'll be with you no matter what."

"I always said, 'Just give me till tomorrow.' We'll find a way to work the rest out."

For the first time, she believed it was possible. She had no idea how, but maybe that was why God hadn't shared yet. "I love you," she said, crying again. "No matter what happens."

"I love you. No matter what happens."

He felt close as her heartbeat—until the click of the disconnect.

Then, Luke felt a million miles away.

Chapter Twenty

It all came down to this.

Luke's heart was pounding against his ribs as he walked up to the chutes. The tight weight of his safety vest, covered in sponsor insignias, felt familiar and yet heavier than usual. He hadn't worn the thing since the day of his accident, and it felt significant to feel it on his chest again. Armor for the battle ahead.

The announcer was making a big sentimental speech about the ride to the audience. Video of his last ride was playing on the screen. The frame froze at the dramatic point of his being thrown from JetPak, mercifully fading to black before he hit the ground in the unnatural twist of limbs that always made his stomach lurch every time he watched it. It wasn't the kind of thing everyone should see. Kids were in the audience. While it was always good PR to hint at the danger of the sport, it was never smart marketing to actually show damage done. "Keep it at the thrill level," Nolan would say while coaching Luke to be tightlipped about the specifics of his injuries over the years.

"A bright, rising star, catapulted into jeopardy earlier this year," the announcer said in dramatic tones. "A man determined to overcome injury and ride again. A true cowboy, a true hero, ready to prove himself today."

Luke used to eat this stuff up. He loved the hyperbole of the rodeo, the spectacle of it all. You couldn't get much larger than life than the man vs. beast battle of bull riding. Today, he found the whole thing a bit overdone. He loved an audience, loved the cheer that roared through the stadium when he walked out into the arena and lifted his hat. He felt their hoots and applause as a nearly physical sensation, a buzz in his chest that seemed to ignite the skills he'd need to last those eight seconds. But the person he wanted most in that audience was miles away. *And right by your side,* he reminded himself, letting his fingers graze over the red bandana.

The live arena camera cut to a shot of Jet-Pak, snorting in the chute behind him. No greenhorn to the theatrics of it all, JetPak tossed his head and bellowed. That animal knew his cue.

Ten minutes ago, Luke had looked the bull square in the eyes. He'd waited for some kind of hate to boil up—it was a useful emotion in the arena—but his feelings only distilled to a sharp competitive focus. Luke had a job to do. JetPak had a job to do. It was only a matter of who came out the victor when those two jobs clashed.

It will be me. This is my moment. This is how I take back what I lost.

Luke walked toward the chutes, giving a moment's thanks for how he no longer limped. The pain he still felt in that leg was his ally, a sign that the sensation had returned. It hurt—stress always made it hurt worse—but Luke could ride with pain. This, he knew how to do. This was his gift.

Dramatic battle music swelled on the PA system, full of pounding drums and tension-building crescendos. The lights in the stands went down, placing the arena in a glow of brightly lit attention. Just before the lights went fully down, Luke cast his glance over to the seats where Gran, Ellie and Nash, Gunner and Brooke, Witt and Jana, and even Audie and Trey sat. He let his gaze linger on the one empty seat next to Ellie, fished the red bandana out of his pocket, and made a show of tucking it next to his heart inside his vest.

See that, Ruby? See me? See you with me? You found a way to be here. That's why we're so good together. That's why we'll make it.

There were no points to be awarded, either for him or the animal. This match had just one measure: eight seconds on, or not enough. No judges analyzing style or control of the animal, just a clock.

Luke climbed up to his place above Jet-Pak, having gone through the near-instinctual process of rosining his bull rope and glove, and picturing his seat on the bull with every jump, twist and spin.

"You know this bull. You know what he does. You've got this," the flank man said as Luke placed each of his feet on the chute rails on either side above JetPak's back. The animal gave a snort and reared up as if he'd heard the flank man's comments and was full bent on challenging them. The guy pulling Luke's bull rope grabbed him by the vest to steady him as the rails shook.

"I think he disagrees," Luke remarked as he began the process of settling his hand into the braided handhold. He adjusted and readjusted, centering his little finger down the spine of the bull. Luke wrapped the rope around his hand, readying himself for the chaos that would be unleashed once the gate was pulled open. He was tired from a poor night's sleep, hurting from his leg's response to the stress, but shot through with adrenaline and surprisingly steady. He could feel the red bandana tucked up against his chest. Sure, every member of the Buckton family carried a turquoise bandana as a sign of their allegiance to the Blue Thorn Ranch, but this was different. This was one man's battle bolstered by one woman's heart.

The gate man, waiting to yank on the rope that would pull the gate open, looked up at Luke for the cue. Luke took a deep breath, lowered his legs and moved up on his rope on the beast, and nodded toward the man. "Outside."

In less than a second, the world began careening in every direction. Luke's well-honed reflexes woke up and took over, his brain making predictions and calculations to shift his body at lightning speed. Time both sped up and slowed down simultaneously, one hand raised high while the core of his body shifted and twisted to match the wild movements of the bull.

It all came down to this.

* * *

Ruby sat in the hospital hallway, cradling her cell phone in her hands as the video streamed in from Ellie's phone in San Antonio. She could hear the Bucktons shouting encouragements. She could hear Granny B praying out loud and in rapid-fire words asking "Lord Jesus, keep that boy on that bull!" which made Ruby laugh.

Her heart had stuck in her throat as he walked up to the chute. Her heart had burst its seams as she watched him deliberately take the red bandana out of his pocket and put it inside his vest. Next to his heart. He must have known she'd see it—the action felt like his own brand of love letter to her. Luke was right—they had found ways to cross the miles toward each other. For the first time, a future for them actually felt possible. Not easy, but possible.

What that future would be, however, might be decided before she took her next breath. The chute was pulled open and JetPak shot out of the gate with Luke on top. She felt Luke's wild movements—not wild at all, she knew now, but carefully orchestrated counterbalances—in her own ribs, felt the jerks of the bull down her own spine.

Two seconds…three seconds…

Her head spun from the tension, the world whittled down to just the jerky image from Ellie's phone as she cheered a hundred and fifty miles away. The arena commentator was saying something but the phone's audio was too scratchy to hear it clearly.

Four seconds…five seconds… *Come on Luke, hang in there…*

Six seconds…seven seconds…so close…

Then everyone made noise and the phone dropped, the screen going dark and jumbled for a moment.

Ruby yelped and stood up, nearly dropping her own phone. Were those cheers? Shouts of alarm? Her entire body seemed to go white like a strobe light—blanked out at high intensity.

She heard Ellie's voice, saw the image of fingers scrambling to pick up the phone. "Sorry," Ellie shouted into the microphone. Then the image focused on the image of Luke, picking himself up off the arena floor, clearly favoring his left leg. The screen panned up to the clock, stopped at seven point five seconds.

Seven point five seconds. *One half of one second* short of the goal.

"He didn't make it," came Audie's voice from the phone speaker, pitched high in alarm.

The arena sounded eerily quiet. After a

breathless couple of seconds, the announcer said something that made the crowd offer a huge, long cheer. Ruby could hear other people cheering, but no sounds from the family members in the row with Ellie.

"Oh, Luke," Ruby heard Ellie's voice. "So, so close."

The phone's camera stayed on Luke, and Ellie watched him straighten up seemingly one slow inch at a time. He picked his hat up off the ground, arm extended up to acknowledge the crowd but eyes cast to the dirt. To watch a man shoulder so great a defeat was a hard thing. Luke stood tall, but the duck of his head went straight to Ruby's heart.

Seven point five seconds. So close. Excruciatingly, achingly close.

"Luke," she found herself touching the phone screen, reaching across the miles with her heart if not her arms. "Oh, Luke." *Oh, Father, why so close? Why so cruel, a half second away?*

Luke's walk out of the arena was slow, deliberate and limping. As if sheer stubborn will was holding him upright and moving. Ruby gulped short, tight breaths, aching alongside him. Defeat looked so ill-fitting on him. He was a man born for victories.

The video stopped, and Ruby heard Ellie's voice. "You there?"

Ruby took the phone off speaker mode, holding it to her ear. "I'm here."

"A half second off." Ellie sounded as if she were holding back tears. "Half a second."

"I saw." The words were dry on Ruby's tongue.

"They're cheering him, Ruby. You should hear how they're cheering him."

"I hear it."

She doubted Luke did.

"Lord have mercy," came Granny B's voice from Ellie's side of the line. For other people, that might have been just an expression. Granny B meant every word of it.

Ruby remembered the image of Luke struggling on that Bosu Balance Trainer, frustrated and desperate for balance against the onslaught of emotion. Back then it was the disappointment of a single insensitive boy. Now a whole arena was cheering his bravery, but she knew the fight to stay upright now was against the onslaught of his own disappointment.

Ellie didn't speak, but kept the phone on. What was there to say?

"I'm sorry..." Ellie finally muttered, but the words sounded as hopeless as Ruby felt.

Sorry for what? That Luke failed? That he tried at all? That he'd been hurt in the first place? That Ruby had gotten caught up in the wave of his attempted comeback? None of these things were anyone's fault. There was no one to apologize to.

"It didn't turn out the way anyone wanted," was all Ruby could come up with. Thin, inadequate words. She really had wanted him to succeed. He seemed to need it so much; she wasn't quite sure what kind of man would be left in the wake of the defeat. "Bring him home." The plea tightened her voice. She couldn't leave—Grandpa was still on the ventilator and Mama was still in pieces—but she could stand by all of them and bear witness to the pain.

"I'll try," Ellie said before ending the call.

Pain. Ruby was bone-weary of pain. Mama was weighted down with the pain of impending loss. Grandpa was suffering from the pain of a failing body. And Luke was wrecked by the pain of losing the thing he thought made him special.

He was wrong, of course. Luke was still special. To God, to his family and to her most of all. Ruby just wondered if she had any hope of getting him to see it.

Mama came out of Grandpa's hospital room

right after the doctor went in. She looked so tired, hugging her sweater to her chest, half-hearted questions in her eyes. "Well?" In quiet tones, by the steady whoosh of Grandpa's breathing machine, Ruby had told Mama the story of what had happened between her and Luke in San Antonio, all the way up to the ride that had ended half a second too soon. She'd poured out everything, even though she didn't think Mama would approve.

As it was, Mama was too spent for disapproval. She smiled at parts, sighed at Ruby's attempts to describe the complicated thing between her and Luke. She closed her eyes and squeezed Ruby's hand when Ruby used the word "love."

To her surprise, the telling seemed to soften her worries. The last few hours had proven to Mama, Ruby hoped, that Luke could not pull her daughter away completely.

"Seven and a half seconds," Ruby repeated. When Mama's weary brain didn't seem to register the significance, Ruby added, "Not enough—it only counts if he lasts for eight seconds." The declaration felt as if it blew a hollow hole in Ruby's chest.

"Sad," Mama said. She sat down on the couch beside Ruby and laid her head on her daughter's shoulder.

That was it, right there. The whole thing was more sad than sorry.

"Your grandfather used to say a man found out who he really was when he pushed up off the bottom." Ruby noticed that Grandpa's wedding ring—the one he never took off—now sat on Mama's index finger. Was that hospital policy? Or had Mama hung on to that piece of Grandpa in case he slipped away?

Most people probably thought Luke had hit the bottom with his accident. She knew better. His bottom was now, when he faced the terrible notion of having to learn who he was when he couldn't do everything. Luke Buckton was about to need a whole new kind of balance.

Let me help him find it, she prayed as she held Mama's hand.

"Mrs. Sheldon?"

Mama looked up at the doctor who had just exited Grandpa's room.

"The fever's broken. The antibiotics are working."

"So…" Mama cued, wanting something more.

"So I think he'll pull through."

Chapter Twenty-One

He'd been so sure. He'd been so wrong.

The whole day became a blur. Luke remembered the noise of the crowd after his ride was over, but it was more like the roar of an impending tornado than any kind of acclamation. The single, lonely memory of him standing in that arena, eyes to the ground, raising his hat in acknowledgment of the crowd because *that's what he had to do*, stuck with his brain and his body like a slipped gear. He physically moved through the actions of leaving the arena and driving out of San Antonio, but his brain neither remembered them or recognized him. It was stuck on that arena floor, frozen in defeat.

There were supposed to be interviews. He'd skipped them, even Rachel's.

People offered hands in support. He shook them, but didn't look anyone in the eye.

Gran hugged him and prayed over him, kissing him on the forehead the way she had when he was a little boy—though now he had to bend down to let her reach. He let her, but it was more resignation than reception.

His leg hurt like it was on fire, his shoulder throbbed where he'd fallen, but it was the hollow of his chest, the sheer airlessness of his lungs, that wounded him most.

One lousy half second. It look longer to sneeze, for crying out loud. Coming so close hurt worse than failing outright. His brain kept replaying that split second where he felt his equilibrium go, when he felt his hand give way and gravity snatched his victory away. *If I could have just hung on one half second longer.* You wouldn't think anger and hopelessness could mix inside a soul, but the pair of them pressed in on him until he felt like a walking echo of himself. The guy who didn't quite pull it off.

He may not have a memory of the time Jet-Pak threw him and gave him those injuries, but now he relished that blank. Wished for it. Because right now it felt as if he'd continually live with the constant reminder of how JetPak threw him and buried him.

That's how it felt. Buried alive. Ellie talked to him the whole drive home—she refused to let him drive on his own, yanking the keys from him and telling her husband, Nash, she'd meet him back in Martins Gap. He was sure she said supportive, comforting things, but the words mostly blew past him like the wind through the truck window. His family was wonderful but they weren't like him. They didn't understand.

They weren't Ruby.

He knew it wasn't fair, but every part of him hated that Ruby wasn't there. While the rest of him was numb and foggy, the need for her was like a fire in the distance, like running for the moon when you could never hope to touch it. Nothing made sense without her to make sense of it for him.

She was his balance. In every way that really mattered. And right now he was so far off balance he felt like he'd never stand up straight again.

When the exit for Martins Gap came into view, he turned to Ellie and said, "Drop me off at Memorial."

"Are you hurt?"

Of course he was hurt. He was crushed beyond recognition, but that's not why he wanted to go to the hospital.

"Oh," she said, understanding. "Sure. But how will you get home?"

Did it matter? There wasn't anywhere in the world he wanted to be right now but near Ruby. Even if she lectured him twelve ways to Sunday, if she chastised him for trying to do the impossible, if she yelled at him for an hour, he still would endure it for the saving grace of being near her.

As Ellie pulled into the blue-white light of the hospital parking lot, she cut the engine and turned to Luke. "I want you to see something before you go."

He leaned his head back against the seat, too airless to put up an argument.

She pulled out her cell phone hit a few buttons, and handed it to him.

It was a text message. From Tess. So his twin sister *had* been watching from halfway around the world in Australia. Somewhere inside Luke recognized that he should feel something about that, or about the fact that she didn't feel like she could text him directly, but nothing could rise to the surface.

Tell Luke 7.5 is more than enough, the text said.

He tossed the phone back onto the truck seat. "What's that supposed to mean?" More than enough to prove he couldn't do it? More than enough to satisfy himself, or God, or whomever? More than enough to say he ought to quit?

"I expect you'll have to figure that out for yourself," Ellie said.

He didn't reply. He simply got out of the car, dimly aware that the sun was setting. She was in there somewhere, and he'd go find her and just be near her.

"Luke," came Ellie's voice, and he turned to see her eyes glistening with tears. "It is, you know. Enough, I mean. She's right."

It was as if his brain couldn't hold the thought. He felt so much "less than" that "enough" just wasn't within reach.

He walked up to the bored-looking woman behind the front desk and said, "Gus Mellows?" He managed a tiny, odd, pop of surprise that he'd remembered Ruby's grandfather was the older brother of the man who used to be the Martins Gap sheriff. The sheriff whom Ellie's new husband, Nash, had replaced. That was the thing about Martins Gap—everybody was connected to everybody somehow. The realization made his disconnected state that much harder to bear. He'd belonged here once, but now he'd spent so much time distancing himself from the place he no longer seemed to fit despite his

Buckton-blue eyes and his Buckton family pedigree. He'd smashed that part of his life to bits and now didn't think he could pick up the pieces.

As if to drive the point home, the attendant said, "It's after visiting hours. Are you a member of the family?"

"No." The word echoed in the vacuum beneath his ribs.

"Then you'll have to wait here."

What did waiting matter? He couldn't go anywhere anyway. Luke walked into the lobby, oddly bright in the evening hours. The starkness suited his mood, despite the attempt at comfortable chairs and warm, welcoming tones. He couldn't sit. He could only stand in the middle of it, holding himself upright with the same stubborn will that held him straight up in the arena. For a man who spent his career in constant motion, defying gravity and brute force, standing still seemed an oddly appropriate task.

The elevator door slid open with a muted scrape, and Ruby saw Luke framed in the arch of the lobby. His back was to her, his hands planted on the wall in front of him as if he needed the paneling to hold him up. It seemed a defeated, almost desperate pose, the opposite of the endless postures of cocky charm he'd been known to adopt. Grandpa's words came back to her: *A man finds out who he really is when he pushes up off the bottom.* She was looking at who Luke really was, stripped of all the bravado and acclaim, grappling himself upright after everything he valued knocked him down.

She loved this man. Not for who he was, or who he wasn't, but for who he was about to become. Luke Buckton rising up from the bottom would be a glorious thing, a rocket like no one had ever seen. Not in any of the ways that everyone expected, but in all the ways that mattered.

Her heart flew across the cold tile floor faster than her feet could manage the run. He turned at the sound of her footsteps, and the tumult in his eyes sunk straight to her heart. A first flash of fear—as if he could ever think she would turn him away now—followed by relief and belonging and happiness and need and everything else that made up love.

She collided with him, not caring that she threw her arms around him so hard she knocked the two of them up against the wall. There was a momentary hesitation—a disbelief she could feel—before his arms wrapped around her. He made a wordless, desperate sound as he sank his face into her hair and clung to her.

She'd once told Mama, in a dramatic high school swoon, that she'd never love again the way she loved Luke. But it was true. Her love for him now was deeper and more true, battle-tested and given with the grace of eyes wide open.

Luke tunneled his fingers through her hair and touched his forehead to hers, his breaths deep and labored. And when he kissed her, it was as if he poured an entire lifetime into it. Sweet and thunderstruck, tender and fierce, it was every kiss they'd ever shared all purified into one.

"How are you?" he asked, eyes still closed, when they finally pulled apart at an overloud cough from the desk attendant.

There was something wondrous in the fact that he had asked her first. Luke could always make her feel like the center of the universe, but back before, it was more of a close orbit around himself. This was a genuine concern, a selflessness she'd never seen from him. "I'm all right," she said quietly, brushing a tousled lock of hair out of his eyes. "He's gonna make it. For now, at least." Ruby ran her hand over his jaw, the stubble of his beard telling her just how long a day it had been. "How are you?"

"I don't know," he admitted, a lost-boy look in his eyes. "Do you?"

The words came to her. "You're done, and just beginning." She shrugged, for the phrase sounded cryptic when she said it aloud.

His brows furrowed. "Sounds complicated."

"Maybe not so much." She kissed the hollow of his throat where his shirt opened, and a kind of release shot through him, an untangling she could feel in his chest and shoulders. A sparkle of delight filled her at the sight of a red bandana corner sticking out of his shirt. She tugged at it, pulling it free. "I was there, beside you even from here."

He settled his arms around her waist. She had always marveled at how perfectly they fit together. Only he winced a bit, reminding her he was likely in pain. "I felt it—you, I mean," he said. "Even at the worst part. And then all I could feel was the distance between us, like I couldn't get a deep breath until I was here." He looked into her eyes. "I couldn't be anywhere but here, even if you wouldn't see me, or yelled at me, or whatever. I had to be near you."

Ruby lay her head against his chest. Even

defeated, he radiated strength. "I know." For a moment, they were silent, leaning against each other up against the wall. She felt his heartbeat against her cheek, felt his arms tighten around her as she held him. "The half second doesn't matter Luke. It's nothing. Let it go."

"Tess said the same thing."

"Tess?" She looked up at him. "You talked to her in Australia?" She knew he hadn't talked to his twin sister nearly enough lately, if at all.

"She sent a text saying 'It's enough.'"

"She's right."

"I want to believe that," he said as he planted a kiss on top of her head and settled her under his chin. He gave a deep and weary exhale. "I'm not sure if I can just yet."

"Do you have to? Just now, I mean?"

"Do you mean can I have faith that it was enough even if I can't quite feel it?"

Ruby stared up at him, surprised to hear such words from him. "Yes," she replied, "I suppose I do."

"Maybe I can. And that's your doing. And God's, I imagine." His hand feathered against her cheek, and she felt the tenderness swell in her heart. "You were always the best thing He ever sent to me, Ruby Sheldon." He kissed her eyelids as she blinked back tears. "You always will be. I'm sorry it took me so long to figure it out."

She invoked another of Grandpa's sayings. "The long way home is still the way home." She wrapped her arms around him more tightly just to prove it.

"You're my home. You're where I belong." He rolled his eyes and grinned. "Cheesy, but true." He winced. "I'm so tired. Ellie wanted to take me home but I knew the only place I wanted to be was here."

Ruby guided him to the set of couches, where he eased himself down with the careful pace of a sore body. He opened his arm and she curled up against him, worn out herself. It was only nine o'clock but it felt well past midnight, as if the hotel alarm clock had blinked its hours years ago instead of just this morning.

"What happened after the ride?" she dared to ask after a moment's blissful quiet.

"I have no idea—I left. There were a dozen interviews lined up but I skipped them all. I've gotten more texts and emails from Nolan in the past hours than I have since I got hurt."

"What do they say?"

He shrugged. "Dunno. Haven't bothered to look at them. For the first time in my life, I wanted to disappear instead of grab the spotlight. Feels weird."

She angled to look up at him. "What will you do now?"

He returned her gaze. "'Don't know that either. He stroked her hair. "Will you help me figure it out?"

She nodded, and he pulled her more tightly against him.

"One thing I know for sure, though."

She felt his heart beat against her cheek, and the remark about him finding his home in her didn't seem so cheesy after all. "What's that?"

"Whatever gets figured out, it'll be us together."

"I like the sound of that."

Chapter Twenty-Two

Ruby watched Luke spread a beautiful afghan over her grandfather's lap as he sat in Mama's living room. "Welcome home, Gus. Ellie knitted this especially for you. And she doesn't whip one of these up for just anyone, you know. After eight weeks in rehab, I reckon you earned this."

Grandpa gave a weak laugh. "I reckon I did. Glad to still be here."

"We're glad to still have you, Pop," Mama said, planting a kiss on Grandpa's head.

Ruby busied herself setting down the bags of Grandpa's things brought back from the rehab center. Oscar, whom Luke had brought to the house for the occasion, gave a "woof" of agreement as he put his paws on Grandpa's knees. Evidently Oscar wanted a welcome home pat from his long-missing buddy. Luke practically lunged for the dog, afraid it'd be too much for the old man, but Ruby smiled as Grandpa waved Luke away and gave Oscar a scratch behind the ears.

"Hey," Grandpa said, peering down at the dog, "what's with the new collar?"

Ruby hadn't even noticed that Oscar now sported a turquoise collar with a big ribbon tied to it in the same color.

"Um," Luke cut in quickly, "that's not for you."

Grandpa squinted closer and got a funny look on his face. "I think you're right." He grinned at Luke, who got an equally funny look on his face.

"Ruby, honey, come get your dog off me," Grandpa said, even though he didn't look at all annoyed that Oscar was eagerly seeking chances to lick his hand.

"Sorry, Grandpa. Here boy!" Ruby called Oscar over, wanting to see what kind of collar Luke had decided her dog needed. She was rather fond of his old one, and couldn't guess why Luke would go off and replace it without asking.

She patted her legs as she sat down, and Oscar leaped onto her lap and began licking her. "Hey there, boy, I've only been gone an hour or two and you got to play with Luke the whole time." She looked down to examine the new collar and gasped. The turquoise leather collar was beautifully hand tooled and personalized with Oscar's name, but that's not why she couldn't breathe.

It was the ring tied to the collar with a bright blue ribbon that stole her breath.

She looked up to find Luke down on one knee in front of her, eyes gleaming, smile as wide as she'd ever seen it. "Oscar and I were busy hatching a little plan this afternoon," he said as he untied the bow to hold the ring up to her. It sparkled in the slanted fall sunlight, and Ruby thought she might tumble off the chair.

"It's been a long time coming, but Ruby Sheldon, I love you. I want to spend the rest of my life loving you. Will you let me?"

"Yes." She wanted to shout the word, but she could only squeak out a whisper. "Absolutely, I'll marry you."

Luke's eyes shone. "Oscar, if you don't mind?" He pointed to the ground and Oscar, evidently all-too-willing an accomplice, hopped obediently down. It gave Luke enough room to lean in and give Ruby a splendid kiss that made the world spin in circles around her. She barely registered the cheers and applause from Grandpa and Mama—evidently they'd both known this was coming.

"I'd have done it sooner—I seriously thought about taking a page from Witt's book and popping the question at his and Jana's wedding last month—but I wanted to wait until the contract came through."

Ruby sat back, her delight doubling. "You got the offer?"

Luke spread his arms. "You're looking at the Rodeo Channel's new commentator for the upcoming season. For three seasons, actually, with an option to extend. I fly in for the televised events, then I fly home for the rest of the time. After the great response to Rachel Hartman's article on my retirement, Nolan said they'd be fools not to take me on. Evidently the man is as good at negotiating entertainment contracts as he is sponsorship deals. He'll probably demand to be a grooms-man at the wedding."

At the wedding. The words glowed in Ruby's chest. "Sure. Why not?"

"Ellie said she's knit you a wedding shawl. Right after she finished her own sets of baby blankets."

"Blankets?" Ruby felt her jaw drop. "You mean?"

"Yep." His grin kept widening. "It's a bumper crop of Bucktons. Twins. Tess says she figures that makes her and me shoo-ins to be the godparents."

Grandpa home, marrying Luke, his new job, babies for Ellie—it felt like more happiness than the world could hold. She didn't even try to stop the happy tears. "I guess so."

Luke reached out and wiped her cheek. "Don't cry, darlin'. You just made me the happiest heart in Texas."

"I beat you to it," she said, lunging out of her chair to throw her arms around Luke as Oscar yapped at their feet. They fell over, a mess of arms and legs and paws and bliss— and nobody cared one bit.

* * * * *

Don't miss these other
BLUE THORN RANCH *stories*
from Allie Pleiter:

THE TEXAS RANCHER'S RETURN
COMING HOME TO TEXAS
THE TEXAN'S SECOND CHANCE

Find more great reads at
www.LoveInspired.com

Dear Reader,

This novel represents our fourth visit to the Blue Thorn Ranch, a place and family I've come to know and love. God has taken each of the Buckton siblings (and their cousin) on journeys of faith and purpose, and it's my prayer that your faith has been strengthened by their stories.

If you've not yet enjoyed the other three books in the series, *The Texas Rancher's Return*, *Coming Home to Texas*, and *The Texan's Second Chance*; please do! There will be one more book in the series coming out in September 2017, so keep watch for it.

As always, I love to hear from readers. You can reach my website at *www.alliepleiter. com*, email me at *allie@alliepleiter.com*, like my Facebook Page at *https://www.facebook. com/alliepleiter*, or connect with me on Twitter at *https://twitter.com/alliepleiter* (@alliepleiter) or Pinterest *http://pinterest.com/ alliepleiter/.* Of course, if good old mail is your thing, you can always reach me at P.O. Box 7026, Villa Park, IL 60181. I'm looking forward to hearing from you!

Get 2 Free Books,
Plus 2 Free Gifts—
just for trying the Reader Service!

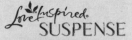

Get 2 Free Books,
Plus 2 Free Gifts—
just for trying the Reader Service!

HOMETOWN HEARTS ♥

YES! Please send me **The Hometown Hearts Collection** in Larger Print. This collection begins with 3 FREE books and 2 FREE gifts in the first shipment. Along with my 3 free books, I'll also get the next 4 books from the Hometown Hearts Collection, in LARGER PRINT, which I may either return and owe nothing, or keep for the low price of $4.99 U.S./ $5.89 CDN each plus $2.99 for shipping and handling per shipment*. If I decide to continue, about once a month for 8 months I will get 6 or 7 more books, but will only need to pay for 4. That means 2 or 3 books in every shipment will be FREE! If I decide to keep the entire collection, I'll have paid for only 32 books because 19 books are FREE! I understand that accepting the 3 free books and gifts places me under no obligation to buy anything. I can always return a shipment and cancel at any time. My free books and gifts are mine to keep no matter what I decide.

262 HCN 3432 462 HCN 3432

Name	(PLEASE PRINT)	
Address		Apt. #
City	State/Prov.	Zip/Postal Code

Signature (if under 18, a parent or guardian must sign)

Mail to the **Reader Service:**
IN U.S.A.: P.O. Box 1867, Buffalo, NY. 14240-1867
IN CANADA: P.O. Box 609, Fort Erie, Ontario L2A 5X3

* Terms and prices subject to change without notice. Prices do not include applicable taxes. Sales tax applicable in NY. Canadian residents will be charged applicable taxes. This offer is limited to one order per household. All orders subject to approval. Credit or debit balances in a customer's account(s) may be offset by any other outstanding balance owed by or to the customer. Please allow 4 to 6 weeks for delivery. Offer available while quantities last. Offer not available to Quebec residents.

READERSERVICE.COM

Manage your account online!

- Review your order history
- Manage your payments
- Update your address

*We've designed the
Reader Service website
just for you.*

Enjoy all the features!

- Discover new series available to you, and read excerpts from any series.
- Respond to mailings and special monthly offers.
- Browse the Bonus Bucks catalog and online-only exculsives.
- Share your feedback.

Visit us at:

ReaderService.com

RS16R